Return of the Crea

RETURN OF CREATURES

By

Richard Terrain

Return of the Creatures

DEEP SPACE.

No atmosphere, no life, nothing. Just a web of lights- a billion stars hang
in a velvet void. The only sound is the howl of the cosmic wind.

The light of a distant sun strikes a rising planet. We see ragged continents and oceans wreathed in cloud. This is earth rise. Our world
spins slowly in space, a thing of beauty, of awesome majesty. In all this
nothingness - life.

We push in on the planet - in to the Americas. The wind grows louder -

A PUEBLO VILLAGE.

A broken-down pick-up bumps into a God-forsaken villages cluster of adobe
houses, blinding flurries of dust and sand. The pick-up stops in front of a
crumbling church. A man in his 60s gets out carrying a medical bag. This is
the DOCTOR. '

Return of the Creatures

A WOMAN'S FACE.

Screaming. She's very young - a South American Indian - lying on a bed in a
corner of one of the houses. She is in the final throes of childbirth, a
sheet draped over her loins. The Doctor works between her legs, encouraging
her in Spanish.

The local PRIEST, not long out of the seminary, crouches at her side
counting off the beads of a rosary. He looks like he is about to pass
out.

SUDDENLY THE WOMAN BITES DOWN HARD ON HER LIP. A THIN LINE OF BLOOD COURSES
DOWN HER CHIN. THE BREATH EXPLODES FROM HER LUNGS AS SHE PUSHES REALLY
HARD
-

DOCTOR

Arriva!

He lifts the child from her loins, but it makes no sound. We don't see the
baby - just the shock on the Doctor's face. The mother struggles up to see

her child.

The Doctor grabs the sheet from her torso and covers the baby with it. He
thrusts the bundle into the Priest's hands.

DOCTOR (CONT'D)

(in Spanish)

Dead - the child is dead. Now go!

We hold on the mother's anguished face. Dissolve to

A HELICOPTER

Off the roof of a tall hospital building. As it rises up into the night we
see a red cross painted on its side. It's an air ambulance.

The chopper turns away. The Manhattan skyline, every skyscraper a blaze of
lights, opens up behind it. The chopper swoops over the Brooklyn bridge and
into the night.

GROVE OF TREES

Winter's coming on - every leaf is a different shade of amber and gold. The helicopter drops down between the branches and lands on an immaculately tended lawn. Surrounding it are the gracious buildings of a great university. Harvard.

Two paramedics clamber out of the back of the helicopter and load a stainless steel casket onto a gurney. They wheel it fast towards one of the buildings. As they go' through the front doors, we hold on a sign etched into the stone

DEPARTMENT OF BIOLOGY

A PAIR OF MECHANICAL HANDS

slide a long cylindrical "key" into the stainless steel casket. We pull back to reveal the casket lies in a sealed, uncontaminated room. A group of people in lab coats -scientists and researchers - stare through the glass walls.

Return of the Creatures

A young TECHNICIAN, working at a console, keyboards in a series of commands.

Sswhish. The top of the steel casket swings open. Clouds of white gas
stream out -whatever's inside has been nitrogen cooled.

The gas clears. Lying inside is the body of a newborn child - except that
the baby has the skin, the face and the features of a man of eighty. The
scientists and the researchers react - shocked.

One of the mechanical hands glides towards the baby. In its fingers it holds a long steel scalpel. This is the highest-tech autopsy you've ever
seen. The scalpel drives down, about to open the chest cavity -

BLOOD SPRAYS

But not from the baby's chest - it's in glass vials, exploding as white-hot
flames consume them. A plastic-gloved lab assistant, silhouetted against

the flames, is emptying hospital waste into a furnace. He slams the door
shut.

He turns we see his face. He's in his 40s, handsome in a rough-hewn way - a
strong jaw and a muscular body. There's a cool intelligence in his eyes,
but a two-day beard and a worn-out uniform make him look like a man who,
between youth and middle-age, lost his way. And so he has. His name is WILL
ROBINSON.

He takes a steel trolley, wheels it through a set of swing doors and out of
sight.

CLOSED CIRCUIT TV SCREEN

features the image of one of the scientists we recognize from the autopsy.
She's in her 30s - attractive, long hair left loose on her shoulders, an
air of authority about her. Her name is BILLIE RAE DIAMOND. She is a
Professor of Biology.

Return of the Creatures

We tilt down from the screen. It hangs from a wall in a deserted laboratory
-overhead lights, rows and rows of wire animal cages. Moving down death
row, feeding the lab animals, is Will Robinson.

TWO SAD-EYED CHIMPS, CLEANING EACH OTHER IN THEIR TINY CAGE, TURN AND STARE
AT HIM. SUDDENLY WILL STOPS - HE'S HEARD SOMETHING ON THE SCREEN THAT HAS
CAUGHT HIS ATTENTION. HE TURNS AND LOOKS -

DIAMOND

The exact cause of death is still unknown. What is certain - we're dealing
with something we've never seen before. Every organ in the body is affected...

Superimposed over Diamond's face is a three dimensional, computer-generated
graphic of the baby's body.

Will forgets about what he's doing. He walks towards the screen. We push in
on it. Screeds of new data appear

Return of the Creatures

```
Vascular System
...............Atrophied

Neurological Function
.........Senile dementia
```

We hold on Will's eyes - he stares at it.

AN AUDITORIUM

Billy Rae Diamond stands on a podium continuing her briefing. About forty scientists are sitting in front of her in a dimly-lit lecture hall.

Diamond is even more impressive in person - she is tall and gracious but you don't become a Professor at Harvard' at her age without having an iron will and a sparkling intelligence. She speaks with great authority -

DIAMOND (CONT'D)

The baby in question, Michael James Flanagan -she points at the computer-generated graphic on a huge screen

was born at New York Hospital yesterday.

Return of the Creatures

MAP OF THE WORLD ILLUMINATES AN ADJOINING SCREEN -

DIAMOND

But the Center for Disease Control in Atlanta has received similar reports
from a village in Bolivia, two cities in Australia, seven countries in
Europe, a cluster of cases in Namibia and Mexico. Forty-two cases in all.

As she speaks, pinpoints of light on the map identify the exact locations.
They dot their way across the entire globe. Dr Diamond turns to face her
audience-

DIAMOND (CONT'D)

Like Michael Flanagan, they were full-term babies. Two hundred and seventy
eight days since conception and yet, by all reasonable medical standards,
they have completed their entire life cycle. They have gone from conception
to death, not in three score years and ten, but in slightly less than nine

months. Michael Flanagan died of old age.

Silence as Diamond lets the scientists and researchers absorb it. On a
balcony high above, another man is taking notes. He sits alone, almost hidden in shadow. It's Will Robinson.

SHEETS OF ICE ON A SHUTTER DOOR

Will crouches in front of a row of self-storage units on the edge of town.
It's night, the place is deserted. He slips a rusted key into a padlock.
Snap! The key breaks.

Will curses. He grabs a piece of timber and pulls a nail out of it. He
slides the nail into the padlock and manipulates the tumblers. The padlock
springs open.

SPIDERS

weave a web in a corner of the storage unit. A work light hangs from the
ceiling. Will is ripping open stacks of boxes from long ago. He puts

together a pile of yellowing files and old floppy disks.

PULLS OUT A CASSETTE TAPE AND STARES AT IT, UNSURE WHAT'S ON IT. HE TAKES A
CASSETTE PLAYER FROM OUT OF THE JUNK, SLIDES IT IN AND PRESSES "PLAY" A HUGE
ROUND OF APPLAUSE. AS IT DIES, WE HEAR A MAN'S VOICE. IT'S WILL, SPEAKING
FROM YEARS AGO -

WILL

(on tape)

I would like to thank the faculty and staff for this great honor...

We push in on Will's face as he listens to himself...

WILL (CONT'D)

have had the opportunity to work with three talented colleagues. I'm privileged to also call them my friends -

A shadow of pain crosses his face. He shuts off the tape and sits motionless.

LAFAYETTE PARK

Return of the Creatures

Night. Homeless people in the park build cardboard shelters against a coming storm. Across the road, the first drops of rain splatter against the
White House.

A string of Government cars pass through the huge gates and pull up in
front of the West Portico. From inside, we hear a man's voice - well-spoken, authoritative

PRESIDENT (O.S.)

There's no mistake - you're sure?

JEFFERSON LIBRARY

Diamond sits in the President's study - book-lined walls, a fire in the
hearth. A group of men sit on the sofasthe Surgeon-General, the Chief of
Staff, the National Security Advisor, the Secretaw of Health. A table is
littered with graphs end files.

DIAMOND

We've got five thousand cases now, Mr President. That's in three weeks. The number is doubling every hundred and sixty-eight hours.

The President stands near a window, half in shadow, the firelight playing
across his face. He's in his 50's but the strain of office makes him look
older.

DIAMOND (CONT'D)

That's a geometric progression, sir. In three months there'll be over seven
million cases. After that we hit the wall -

She pushes a thick, bound volume across the table.

DIAMOND (CONT'D)

According to this, there won't be a live birth on the planet.

The President looks at her for a moment. Then he reaches down and picks up
the bound volume. It's hundreds of pages of numbers and projections.

PRESIDENT

These are just computer projections -

species don't disappear that fast.

DIAMOND

Tell that to the dinosaurs, sir.

He looks out the window at the winter storm sweeping down on them.

NATIONAL SECURITY ADVISOR

What date - when exactly do we hit this wall?

DIAMOND

Six months and twenty-one days.

Silence. The President keeps looking out the window.

PRESIDENT

Can't somebody tell me - what exactly are we dealing with. Is it a virus or
what?

DIAMOND

We don't know, sir.

The President turns to the Chief of Staff.

PRESIDENT

Whatever they need, Bob - anything. Harry Truman put together the Manhattan
Project - you understand?

The Chief of Staff nods his head - yes.

PRESIDENT (CONT'D)

(softly)

A world without children -it's inconceivable. And what about the rest of us
- what do we do? Just sit and watch our species die? Will the last person
to leave the planet turn out the lights.

Silence again. Finally a young woman - the White House Press Secretary -
speaks.

PRESS SECRETARY

We're going to have to manage the public. Right now, the truth may be inoperative -

PRESIDENT

Return of the Creatures

Of course we're going to have to manage itl We're going to have to manage a
whole lot of things. But can't we take at least one moment to be human?

He looks around the room. We hold on their somber faces.

A CHEAP APARTMENT

Through the window - the neon sign of a gas station. This is Will's place,
He lives alone - a bed in the corner, run-down furniture, dishes in the
sink.

The kitchen table has been turned into a desk - Will sits at an old computer, surrounded by the yellowing stacks of files and floppy disks. He
stares at the screen - the notes and equations are blurred. He's been at
this so long, he can barely focus. He rubs his hand across his eyes.

A small mewing sound. Will turns to an alcove in the corner - a cat lies in
a basket, panting. Will goes to her.

Return of the Creatures

She's giving birth - the first of her new-born kittens lies next to her.
Will strokes the mother's head, looking at the miracle of new life. He puts
his fingers in a water bowl, about to moisten the mother's mouth.

Then he stops. He looks again at the kitten - there's two of them now. A
beat as he just stares -

WILL

(softly)

Jesus Christ... of course!

A LUXURIOUS BATHROOM

Through frosted glass we see the silhouette of a woman taking a shower.
Whoever she is, she's got a great figure. The sound of a doorbell. The
shower door opens -Diamond sticks her head out. She looks at a clock - it's
almost midnight.

VIDEO ENTRY PHONE

A video screen monitors the front door. On it we see Will - his hair

tousled, an old overcoat buttoned to the neck, a battered briefcase under
his arm.

Diamond - a towel around her shoulders, hair dripping - picks up the phone.

DIAMOND

Who is it?

WILL (O.S.)

Will Robinson.

DIAMOND

I think you have the wrong house.

WILL (O.S.)

I work at the department.

He turns and looks straight into the camera. Instinctively, Diamond covers
her breasts. She looks at him - recognition dawns.

AN ELEGANT ROOM

Will and Diamond sit in the living room of a gracious townhouse - wooden

floors and beautiful rugs. Diamond doesn't wear any make-up -just jeans and
an oversized shirt. She looks even more beautiful. It does nothing to ease
Will's nerves. He's got his briefcase open in front of him, speaking from
sheaves of notes and papers.

DIAMOND

(interrupting)

Hold on - how do you know about the case load? The Government's trying to
manage this - they've withheld that information.

WILL

The Internet, Doctor. It's a highway - you can ride it anywhere you want. I
got into 'the Center for Disease Control. I had a look at their raw data.

DIAMOND

Jesus. Do you know what you're doing? This is the White House we're talking
about.

WILL

(Heated))

No, it's a disease and it doesn't come any worse than this - that's what
we're talking about.

HE LOOKS AWAY, CALMING HIMSELF. HE SHUFFLES HIS NOTES. HE SPEAKS AGAIN,
QUIETLY -

WILL

I've listened at the lab - I think I know where you're looking. Bacterias
mostly, but there's a strong push into the retro-viruses. You're wrong,
Doctor.

DIAMOND

Really - and I thought I was arrogant. But then, I'm just a professor.

WILL

No virus or bacteria has ever discriminated on the grounds of sex.

DIAMOND

I can think of one.

WILL

Sure, it can start in pockets but it never stays there. This thing does. It
only affects women of child-bearing age. What - it's so smart it can recognize motherhood? I don't think so. No, this is into the very heart of
what we are. This is genetic. This is part of the DNA.

DIAMOND

Thank you. A hundred thousand genes make up human DNA - that really narrows
it down.

WILL

As a matter of fact it does. There's only one part of the DNA that's passed
exclusively through women. Thirty-seven genes, the oldest part of the human
organism -

DIAMOND

(realizing)

The mitochondrial DNA.

WILL

Over the years there's been speculation -not all of it crazy either - that somehow it triggers aging, He slides a sheaf of yellowing extracts from scientific journals across the table. She doesn't pay them any attention - she's thinking.

DIAMOND

You realize what you're saying, don't you? A bacteria - I think we'd get it for sure. A virus -you'd have to say we've got a chance. But say you're right. The mitochondrial DNA - that's so far out on the frontier, we can barely see it.

WILL

Like I said - it doesn't get any worse than this.

She keeps staring down at the documents and notes lying on the table. A beat.

WILL (CONT'D)

Are you okay?

DIAMOND

Sure.

WILL LOOKS AT HER FOR A MOMENT -

WILL

Shit. You're pregnant, aren't you?

DIAMOND

Nine weeks.

THEIR EYES MEET - SHE SHRUGS, TRYING TO PUT A BRAVE FACE ON IT. SHE GETS TO HER FEET -

DIAMOND

Do you want a drink - coffee, a sandwich or something?

WILL

(Recoiling)

No...no, I'm fine thanks.

Watches as he picks up his papers and puts them back in his battered briefcase.

AN EMPTY STREET

It's late at night. Will clutches his briefcase under his arm, heading
home. A bitter wind blows out of the north. He looks a lonely and forlorn
figure as he makes his way through the pools of light cast by the streetlights.

CONVOY OF N.A.S.A. TRUCKS

RUMBLE THROUGH THE EARLY MORNING - THE CITY IS JUST WAKING. THE TRUCKS,
DOZENS OF WHITE EIGHTEEN-WHEELERS, TURN THROUGH THE FRONT GATES OF HARVARD.
THEY STOP IN FRONT OF THE GROVE OF TREES. WE CRANE UP FROM THEM TO A WINDOW
IN THE BIOLOGY BUILDING -

HAND HITS A TABLE

IT'S DIAMOND - SHE'S ANGRY. BREAKFAST TRAYS CLUTTER THE TABLE - SHE'S IN THE
MIDDLE OF A CONFERENCE WITH A GROUP OF SCIENTISTS. SHE GLARES AT AN ARROGANT YOUNG NEUROLOGIST -

DIAMOND

                    It's just an idea, Bob. All we're
                    doing is taking it for a walk
                    around the
                    block.

                    A man in his 60s - distinguished,
                    diplomatic - intercedes.

                    DE MAUPASSANT

                    There was a lot of work done on it
                    in the 70s. I can't recall the
                    details
                    but someone had the idea that
                    mitochondriel DNA was like a
                    genetic memory.
                    If you could unlock it, you could
                    physically travel back down it.
                    Through
                    evolution - like a time machine.

                    BOB

                    Wow! Those 70s, man. I'm really
                    sorry I missed them.

                    Everyone - Diamond included -
                    laughs.

                    OLD PHOTOS OF A SAILING BOAT

                    They hang on the wall of a tiny
                    room - not an office, just a
                    hole-in-the-wall Will has turned
                    into his own. He sits at a table,
                    making

notes. A knock - Diamond enters.

DIAMOND

I thought you'd like to know - we're looking at mitochondrial DNA,

WILL

Thanks for telling me.

THEY LOOK AT ONE ANOTHER. IT'S AN AWKWARD MOMENT - NEITHER ONE QUITE SURE
WHETHER OR HOW TO CONTINUE THE CONVERSATION. DIAMOND SEES THE PHOTOS -

DIAMOND

Is that you?

She points at a man in his 20s standing on the deck in one of the photos,
Will nods.

DIAMOND (CONT'D)

Seattle. Is that where you went to school?

Will hesitates - we sense that he doesn't really want to answer.

WILL

No. Princeton.

DIAMOND

Expensive.

WILL

A scholarship. Then I did some post-graduate work... I never really finished.

Something in the way Will says it - some sense of loss - makes Diamond pause. She recovers and looks in her wallet. She pulls out a photograph and hands it to Will. It shows a small sailing boatgaff-rigged and a varnished hull.

WILL (CONT'D)

It's a Kestrel 24 - I haven't seen one of those in years. She's a beautiful boati

DIAMOND

My grandfather left it to me. I don't sail it much any more - it's too hard to find a for'etd hand.

Return of the Creatures

WILL

What about your husband - doesn't he sail.

DIAMOND

I don't know - I haven't met him yet.

WILL LOOKS AT HER. HIS EXPRESSION SAYS IT - WHAT? SHE SHRUGS -

DIAMOND

I wanted a baby but I'm thirty-four-years old. Sooner or later you realize
that somewhere along the way you've missed the man you've been waiting for.

WILL

What did you do - ask a friend?

DIAMOND

I thought of it.

WILL

Lucky friend.

DIAMOND

I went to a clinic. Not exactly
romantic, but it worked.

(pauses)

Good idea, bad timing.

WILL

How many people have you put on the
mDNA?

DIAMOND

Seven.

WILL

That's all?!

DIAMOND

That's all I can spare. It's just a
theory -one of dozens of theories.

Will looks away in disgust.

DIAMOND (CONT'D)

What is it with you - it's not just
science is it? Why are you so
passionate about this?

WILL

I know I'm right. It's a mutation.
A hundred thousand years it's probably
been lying there -shifting, weaving
into the mDNA. You either go back and
change evolution or you engineer it
out. Seven peopleYou might as well
shoot peas at a dam.

DIAMOND

You haven't answered my question -
why so passionate?

WILL

The question's not relevant. The
only thing I'm interested in is the
science.

He turns back to his work. We hear
the door close as Diamond leaves.

A GEODESIC DOME

White, space-age, is being erected
on the lawn. Workmen are unloading the
NASA trucks. We pull back through a
high window of the Biology building. A
woman stands there, looking out.
Her name is KRIS McQUADE. This is her
office -

Return of the Creatures

MCQUADE

You want to tell me what's going on?

She turns and looks at Diamond, sitting on the other side of the desk,

DIAMOND

Don't ask, Kris, I'd have to lie and I don't want to do that to my best
friend,

MCQUADE

The rumor is, you've done something really big. They say the Defense Department is taking it over.

Diamond just sits there, staring straight ahead. McQuade waits. Finally -

MCQUADE (CONT'D)

Okay, okay - I'm sorry I asked. So what about this guy - what's he done?

DIAMOND

He hasn't done anything - I'm just interested.

MCQUADE

Ten thousand employment records
I've got on file and you want to
know about
a lab assisant?

DIAMOND

The smartest assistant I've ever
known.

MCQUADE

What - he can mop and fart at the
same time?

She picks up pages from a computer
printer - including a copy of
Will's
photo I.D.

MCQUADE (CONT'D)

He's handsome, at least I'll say -

(a thought strikes her)

Jesus - you're not interested in
him like that, are you?

DIAMOND

No, but he's the most unbelievable
smelling man.

MCQUADE

Smelling? You're pregnant -
obviously your hormones have gone
crazy. What
exactly does he smell like?

DIAMOND

You know...

(searching for the right word)

.., wholesome.

MCQUADE

Of course he does - that's the
Lysol.

Diamond laughs but McQuade barely
notices it. She's leafing through
WiU's
file -

MCQUADE (CONT'D)

That's strange - there's supposed
to be a background sheet. Family,
school
-all that shit. It must have gotten
lost.

Before Diamond can say anything, a
young man enters. He's McQuada's
assistant.

ASSISTANT

Your secretary's on the line, Dr Diamond. There's a call for you.

DIAMOND

Tell her to take a message.

ASSISTANT

It's the New York Times.

MCQUADE

What do they want?

DIAMOND

I think Washington's news management just went south.

THE WHITE HOUSE

Night. Scores of television news vans are parked outsideDutch, Japanese and
French reporters are doing stand-ups live-to-air. We hear Peter Jennings of
ABC.

JENNINGS (O.S.)

We're standing by to go live to Washington as events continue to unfold on

this remarkable day. I don't think
there's a person anywhere who's not
sitting by a radio or television
now. I'm told the President is on
his way
to the press room -

FIFTH AVENUE

is totally empty - just a young man
on rollerblades. He skates
effortlessly
down the deserted avenue - past
Tiffany's and the Trump Tower, all
silent
now.

PRESIDENT (O.S.)

My fellow Americans...

The rollerblader passes the
cathedral of St John. The front
doors are open.
Someone is playing the organ -
Mozart's Requiem. The rollerblader
fades
into the night.

STEEL DOOR OPENS

A sharp-faced caretaker - scruffy
clothes and a limp - escorts Will
into a
vaulted basement. All we can see
are silhouettestowers of crates,
racks of

Return of the Creatures

equipment...

CARETAKER

This used to be the basement of the Psychology Department. We just sort of
stacked everything around 'em -

He flicks a switch - the storage room floods with light. He points at two
long iron cylinders - like small submarines - rigged up to a series of
valves and pipes.

CARETAKER (CONT'D)

Flotation tanks. They used 'em for experiments in sensory degradation -

WILL

Deprivation - sensory deprivation.

CARETAKER

Yeah, well - whatever.

SHAFT OF LIGHT

WILL OPENS AN IRON HATCH THAT GIVES ACCESS INTO ONE OF THE TANKS. HE DROPS

INTO IT AND WALKS FORWARD,
EXAMINING IT. THE DARKNESS CLOSES
AROUND HIM. HE
STARES AHEAD. VOICES DRIFT OUT OF
MEMORY -

YOUNG MAN (O.S.)

Now I know what a mole feels like -

YOUNG WOMAN (O.S.)

(lightly)

It feels like a fucking coffin,
that's what it feels like.

Other voices laugh. They're all
young and like the young they think
they'll
never die.

CARETAKER (O.S.)

Hey, fella - what are you doing?

HE'S PEERING DOWN THROUGH THE
HATCH. WILL DRAGS HIMSELF OUT OF
THE PAST. HE
TURNS -

WILL

Just looking. I'll be coming back -
I'll need a key.

Return of the Creatures

The caretaker shrugs - sure. Will climbs out of the tank.

WILL (CONT'D)

One other thing - don't tell anyone, huh?

CARETAKER

Who would I tell? They treat me like shit Worse than shit. All work, no
appreciation. The phantom of Harvard. Someone should write a fucking
musical about me.

CIRCLES OF LIGHT

Desk lamps, glowing in an office. Diamond and a team of researchers are
working through piles of old journals and extracts from scientific papers.

RESEARCHER

Here's another one - "Mitochondrial DNAA Map to the Past."

DIAMOND

Who's it by?

RESEARCHER

Same guy - Doctor Robert Plant.

DIAMOND

Jesus, what did this guy do - write the book on it? Who is he?

HUGE BOOK BEING OPENED

It's a scientific directory. The researcher flicks the pages and stops at
"Plant".

RESEARCHER

Wow - I thought your career was impressive.

Diamond looks up from her reading.

RESEARCHER (CONT'D)

Degrees in medicine and microbiology. A PhD at 24, a member of the Academy
of Sciences, published twenty times by 1974...

DIAMOND

And then?

RESEARCHER

Then nothing.

DIAMOND REACTS. SHE GETS TO HER
FEET, COMING CLOSER -

DIAMOND

Where did he go as an
undergraduate?

RESEARCHER

Princeton.

DIAMOND

On a scholarship?

A CORRIDOR

It's late at night. The scientists
and their staff are working around
the
clock. Will wheels a trolley laden
with bottles, vials, and catheters
down
a crowded corridor. Diamond pushes
through the people behind, trying
to
catch up to him. Scientists turn to
speak to her but she ignores them.

DIAMOND (CONT'D)

Robert!

Will keeps walking, heading for an elevator. Diamond skirts around a knot
of people.

DIAMOND (CONT'D)

Doctor Plant!

Will hesitates - one split second - then keeps going. The elevator doors
slide open. Will steps in, turns and hits a button. He watches Diamond
pushing towards him. For a moment their eyes meet. She comes closer. Sswhish! The doors slide shut.

DIAMOND'S OFFICE

She sits behind her desk, listening to the chief of campus security.

SECURITY OFFICER

The equipment you saw him with was taken from three labs. It includes a
range of genetic material-

(hands her an inventory)

We've checked all the buildings your team is using - he's not in any of
them.

Return of the Creatures

DIAMOND

What about hie house?

SECURITY OFFICER

He asked his landlady to look after his cat. She hasn't seen him for three
days.

IN THE BASEMENT

there's a make-shift bed and a hot-plate with a battered saucepan. Next to
it is a rack of medical equipment and laboratory vials.

Will is sit'ting in front of three computers running in parallel -
data and
equations reel across them. The caretaker comes out of the shadows, carrying two mugs of thick coffee. He puts one down next to Will -

CARETAKER

You wanna tell me what exactly you're doing?

WILL

Looking for a date.

The caretaker stares at the confusion of diagrams and equations on the
screen -

CARETAKER

What's wrong with a calendar?

WILL

These are chemical sequences - they represent human genes. By following a
trail of mutations, I can date them. I'm trying to find out when a major
change occurred in something called the mitochondrial DNA.

CARETAKER

The mitochondrial DNA? Yeah... well that makes sense.

But Will barely hears it. Suddenly he's leaning forward, keyboarding in
complex commands. The caretaker watches him -

CARETAKER (CONT'D)

You've found it?

WILL

Return of the Creatures

Maybe...

He has illustrations of two long-chain molecules on the screen. He moves
them together. Aa they overlap, we see they're not identical - the tail of
one kicks upwarda. Will starel at it -

WILL (CONT'D)

(softly)

Yeah - I've found it.

CARETAKER

So - what's the date?

Will presses a key. Faster than the eye can follow, the first long-chain
molecule starts to shift and mutate. Finally it resolves itself into the
second molecule. Will looks at a graph on the side of the screen -

WILL

The best computer science can do? One hundred and two thousand years ago.

CARETAKER

Sort of what I figured - give or take a day or two.

DIAMOND'S OFFICE

Diamond is poring through scientific articles written by Will. She flicks a
page -there's a photo of Will, 20 years younger, surrounded by three colleagues. He's got his arm around one of them - an attractive young woman.

Diamond lifts the photo, looking at it more closely. She starts to read the
caption. We push in on it and hold on the words... "UC Berkeley".

WE ARE FLYING

swooping and soaring - through a weird landscape of towering cliffs, tumbling streams and primordial forest. There's something unreal about it -
we pull back to reveal they're computer-generated images, playing on the
screens in the basement.

The caretaker has pulled up a chair. He and Will are watching the images
generated by a CD-ROM.

WILL

This is someone's version of the prehistoric world. I'm interested in the
geography, the atmosphere -that sort of stuff.

CARETAKER

Where are we?

WILL

Africa - that's where Mankind started.

Will keeps looking at the strange images. The caretaker gets to his feet -

CARETAKER

I'll see you in the morning.

WILL

Yeah.

The caretaker limps towards the door. Will looks up -

WILL (CONT'D)

Thank you - for helping me, I mean.

Return of the Creatures

CARETAKER

It sounds like you're leaving or something.

WILL

No. I just wanted to say it, that's all.

The caretaker keeps looking at him -

CARETAKER

What exactly are you doing? You're a bit old to try and make your mark,
aren't you? Anyway, nobody listens to people like us.

WILL

Fate can be kind - sometimes a man gets a second chance. Do you know what
it's like to be ridiculed, to have your ideas thrown back in your face? And
that was the easy part. I guess that's what I'm doing - I want to prove
that I was right.

CARETAKER

You're lying to me.

WILL

What do you mean?!

CARETAKER

You are going somewhere. I don't know where it is. I'm not even sure I can
imagine it. Good luck, though. I hope you find whatever it is you're looking for.

WILL

Thanks.

CARETAKER

No point in getting you breakfast, huh?

Will shakes his head - no. They smile at each other. The caretaker turns
and goes.

DIAMOND'S OFFICE

Diamond looks up from the papers and articles littering her desk. Her
Secretary stands in the doorway -

SECRETARY

Return of the Creatures

I've got Eleanor Wilkins on the phone. She runs the archives at Berkeley.

DIAMOND

(into phone)

Ms Wilkins?

We push in tight on Diamond's face as she listens. Anxiety and alarm register on it.

OUTER OFFICE

The security officer and several of his men are looking at maps of the campus. Researchers and scientists have gathered in the office, rumors are
flying. Everyone turns - Diamond stands in the doorway to her office. She
looks at deMaupassant.

DIAMOND (CONT'D)

You were right, Luc. That work you remembered from Berkeley - he was the
one that did it. He said man was the last step on an evolutionary trail.
Within every one of us is the history of our race. It's imprinted on our

genes - like a map. Anyone that can find the chemical key can travel back
down it. Through the womb. Through time and space -

(she looks at them all)

That's what he's doing. He's going back. He's going to try and change evolution.

SECURITY OFFICER

Is that possible?

DIAMOND

He was the best of his generation. He thinks so. He's got the genetic material for the key. All he needs are flotation tanks.

THE FLOTATION TANKS

The valves are open - warm water is pouring into the tanks.

Will sits next to the rack of medical equipment, beads of sweat on his
forehead. He slides a syringe into his forearm and inserts a catheter. He
opens a series of tiny valves on the glass vials. A cocktail of fluid -

minutely measured doses - flows
down the clear plastic towards his
arm. The
fluid hits his blood stream and
drains into it.

A LONG CORRIDOR

Diamond and the others run fast
through pools of light cast by
naked bulbs.
Ahead -a pair of swing doors -

BOB

A theory's one thing - do you
really think he'll try it?

DIAMOND

He's spent fifteen years as a lab
assistant. He lives in a two room
walk-up
with a cat. No family, no friends.
What's There's left for him here?
Of
course he'll do it.

Smack! They push through the doors,
into another corridor.

AN IRON LADDER

Will climbs up the side of the
flotation tank. Suddenly he stops -
a

tremor, a rippling wave, passes from his feet to his head. It's his muscles
contracting. It wracks him with pain. He gasps at the intensity of it.

Smash! The steel door into the basement shudders as someone tries to get
in. Will looks up - the door twists and moves. His vision is starting to
distort. He grabs the access hatch and swings through -

Splashl He drops into the water. Clang! He closes the hatch.

Barn? The steel door flies open. The security officer lowers a sledge
hammer. Diamond steps in end throws a light switch.

DARKNESS IN THE TANK

Will floats on his back, the only sound is the rapid thump of his
heartbeat. The water sloshes back and forth - his muscles are going into
spasms. We push along his body - up to his face. His eyes roll back into
his headl

Return of the Creatures

All we see are the whites of them. They shatter into a web of capillaries -

WILL'S POV

red mist swirls in front of him. It resolves itself into a web of interwoven tendrils -the double helix of the DNA molecule. Will starts to
travel through it -

INSIDE THE TANK

Will is morphing, shedding cells - we're losing him in the warm, dark fluid
of the tank. It's like the womb. His body seems to be disintegrating,
dissolving into it. Water flows through the sockets where his eyes once
were.

His hollow mouth opens. From far away we hear him scream - a primal scream.

OUTSIDE THE TANK

Not a sound escapes. The security officer is about to try and open the
hatch.

Return of the Creatures

DIAMOND (O.S.)

NO!

The security officer turns - Diamond is holding the catheter in her hand.

DIAMOND (CONT'D)

If we open the hatch, I think we'll kill him. It's too late - it's his journey, he's going to have to take it.

INSIDE THE TANK

Will's body is like a shadow, almost one with the water, growing less
distinct by the moment. What is left of his face - a strange, shifting
shape - floats towards us. Closer... closer. It melts completely into the
water -

WILL'S POV

He spirals down a tunnel - into a whirlpool of white light. As he hits, it
shatters into a million fragments of light. It looks like a comet, wheeling

through the heavens. A cosmic wind
blows it forward. Will is traveling
through space and time -

OUTSIDE THE TANK

Diamond and the others are gathered
around the computers. Bob is working
the keyboard. Diamond is
looking.through the piles of
papers, notes and
star charts.

DIAMOND

Everything's here - he kept a
record of every step. He can even
tell the
date -forty hours after he arrives
there's a solar eclipse.

BOB

Billie - there's a note for you.

Diamond looks over his shoulder at
the computer screen. She reads what
is
writ'ten -

DIAMOND

"I won't be here, but if I solve
this thing make sure you tell them,

Return of the Creatures

Billie. Tell them it was Robert Plant, Doctor Robert Plant of UC Berkeley."

THE FRAGMENTS OF LIGHT

blaze through the heavens. They draw together, changing and reconstituting
into a shape we recognize - the interwoven strands of DNA molecules. The
strands connect. A blast of light! It's the rays of -

THE SUN

streaming into a cave. Will lies in the fetal position, bleeding from his
nose and ears. The light grows stronger - it's dawn. Will drags himself up
and stumbles towards the entrance. We tilt up from him. He doesn't see it,
but we do - prehistoric cave paintings are etched into the rock.

A CRAGGY PEAK

Will steps out of the cave. Sunrise sweeps over a world born brand new -
plains and jungle and primordial forest. Rising above it is a snow-capped

mountain that looks like
Kilamlnjlro. A ragged gash runs across the earth -
a rift valley. Will stares at it. He raises his face to the sun. He did it.
The first step's over - and he did itl He looks down - rising out of the
valley is a tiny pillar of smoke.

A FOREST CLEARING

In the middle are the smoldering remains of a camp-fire. Will moves cautiously towards it. He stops - several bodies, terribly mangled, lie on
the ground.

Will turns one of them over - he's got matted hair, a heavy brow and a short, muscular body. As primitive as he is, there's no doubt of his species. He is a man. A Paleolithic man.

This was a hunting party -scattered weapons and the trussed carcasses of
dead animals lie nearby. For a moment Will thinks the hunters must have
been torn apart by wild animals. Then he looks up into the trees - more

Return of the Creatures

bodies of the hunters. But no
animal did this - they hang from
iron chains,
left there as some sort of trophy.
Or a warning.

CRUSHED LEAVES AND BROKEN PLANTS

Will is following a tiny trail
through the forest. He's taken what is
useful from the bodies of the
hunters - an otter-skin water bag, two
short-handled spears and a bed-roll
made from an animal pelt. He moves on -
deeper into the shadows of the
forest.

A SPARKLING STREAM

Will splashes through the crystal
water. He looks upstream - a small lake.
A flock of strange birds - like
huge flamingos take flight in a blaze of
pink and gold.

He steps out of the stream and
along a path beneath a canopy of
over-arching trees. We hold on his
feet - whip! He triggers something.
A

net of woven vines engulfs him. He
drops the spears and bedroll.
Suddenly
he's soaring through the air.

He jerks to a halt - he's a netted
animal hanging high in the trees.
The
faces of two Paleolithic men,
crouched on boughs, stare at him.

PLUME OF WATER

cascades a hundred feet into a
hidden gorge. Smoke curls up from
fires.
Scores of stone-age people - man,
women and children - turn and look.
Will,
roped and bound, is being hauled
into the encampment.

The primitive people - nervous but
intrigued - circle around him. They
are
dressed in skins and fur. talismans
hang from their necks. The warriors
carry not only weapons but ritual
scars across their foreheads. It
makes
them look even more savage.

Will is led past the haunches of
soma massive animal cooking in a
pit. A
pile of ivory tusks lie nearby. The
two captors jerk on the leash - it

Return of the Creatures

stops Will in front of a cave.
Hanging from the roof is the giant
pelt and
head of their totema saber-toothed
tiger. This is the Tribe of the
Tiger.

A man emerges from under its
outstretched paws. He's in his late
20's -
proud and strong. His name is Kip-
Kena - he is their leader. He and
Will
look at one another.

Kip uses his hands to sign to Will
in the formal language of his race.
Will
stares at him - he has no idea what
it means. He shrugs. Kip tries a
new
tack - he speaks. The sounds are
rough and guttural - but
understandable,
KiP Where is your tribe?

Will pauses, searching for an
answer- where do you start? He
gives up.

WILL

I don't have a tribe.

A rolling murmur of disbelief from
the surrounding tribe.

Return of the Creatures

KIP

No man can live without a tribe!
How would he hunt the mighty
animals? Who
would keep his fire burning?

WILL

I come from far away... I'm a
traveler.

KIP

What is traveler? Is that a tribe?

Again Will's at a loss. Something
catches Kip's eye. He reaches
forward and
rips the water bag out from under
Will's coat. The tribe reacts -

KIP (CONT'D)

You carry things taken from our
hunters! Kill him.

He turns away. Will throws himself
at him -

WILL

NO!

Whackl A blow to the back of Will's
neck knocks him to his knees. He
looks

Return of the Creatures

up -two warriors have their spears
raised, about to plunge them into his
chest.

A sound like thunder - it's hooves.
The warriors turn. Will follows their
gaze - half an army, mounted on
horseback, surges into the gorge,
They are
heavily armed, dressed in armor but
it's not their weaponry that
astonishes
Will. These are apes!

The tribes-people scream in terror.
They turn and run. The two warriors
forget about Will. He dives for
cover in a pile of rocks. As he tears
himself free of the ropes that bind
him, he looks out -

The apes charge in to the camp. At
their head is a huge gorillarippling
muscles and intelligent eyes - deep
set and yellow, like pissholes in the
snow. He wears a suit of black
armor ribbed in silver. His name is
Drak. He
is the Lord of the High Rivers,
supreme commander of the ape army.
On

either side ride his elite
Praetorian Guard.

Woo-woo-woo! Kip swings a hollow
piece of wood above his head. It's a
bull-roarer. The warriors of the
tribe know its meaning - they rally to
Kip's side. Armed only with spears
and primitive bows they stand between
the apes and their panic-driven
people, trying to buy them time to get into
the cave.

Sswhish! The sound of arrows. The
apes carry triple-barreled iron
crossbows.

Short iron bolts cut several of the
tribesmen down. Dust and smoke swirls
across the camp. Kip and his men,
fighting all the way, retreat towards the
cave.

A baby's cry! Will turns - a
toddler sits at a hearth, left
behind in the
confusion. Will half rises to his
feet, about to go for him. Too late -

Return of the Creatures

there's a blur of movement irt the
trees. A tribe-boy - too young to be a
warrior - has come back for the child.

Out of the dust and smoke - Drak!
Foam flies from his horse's mouth. He's
seen the boy and the child. He locks what looks like a Gatling gun tight
under his huge bicep.

Will screams a warning. The boy turns - he sees Drak as he fires. A hail of
iron darts - twenty or more - cut him and the child down.

Rage flashes in Will's eyes. He scrambles over a boulder and rips a crossbow from a dead ape's hand. He slides bolts into the barrels and grabs
a lever with both hands -you need the strength of an ape to cock it. A
sound behind him - little more than a whisper. He swings -It's an arrow.
Whackl It rips into his shoulder, hurling him to the ground. Ape infantry -
foot soldiers - are coming into the gorge behind him.

Return of the Creatures

In their midst are three huge steam-driven machines - like iron erector
sets. One is the Claw, one is the Balls and the other is the Flame.

THE CAVE ENTRANCE

Kip and his warriors have seen them too. They scramble into the cave. Men
and women are inside, swinging closed two huge stockade doors made from
tree trunks.

Other warriors, caught outside, run for the closing gap. On their heels is
Will - still clutching the crossbow, blood streaming from his wound. The
doors are closing... closing. Will dives through the gap, almost crushed -

INSIDE THE CAVE

Slam! The doors fly shut. Wham! A huge cross-beam drops into place. Will,
sprawled in the dust, looks up - chaos. By torchlight, the medicine man is
tending the wounded, children are screaming, women and old people are

Return of the Creatures

clambering up a series of ledges.
High above is a tiny slash of
daylightanother entrance.

From deep in the cave Will hears
the roar of some animal but he
doesn't
have time to think about it. Smash!
The great wooden doors shudder from
some mighty blow.

OUTSIDE THE DOORS

The three machines are in place.
The first of them has two huge
stone balls
suspended by chains from an
overhead jib. An ape sits right on
top,
operating it. The balls dance and
swing wildly - smash! They hit the
door,
opening a hole.

INSIDE THE CAVE

Daylight streams in. Kip and his
warriors have ranged themselves
high
around the walls, ready to attack
when the apes pour in. A pair of
huge
iron jaws appear in the hole. This
is the second of the apes' machines
-
the Claw.

Return of the Creatures

Another roar from the animal. Will watches the Claw reach in and grab the
massive crossbeam. It snaps it like a twig. Will gets to his feet and runs.
He sees Kip signal -

AN OLD WARRIOR

is perched high on a series of wooden bars that seal off a corner of the
cave, turning it into a cage. He opens it.

Crash! The stockade doors at the front of the cave burst open. The first of
the ape cavalry charges in. A roar from the unseen animal. The apes' horses
catch the scent of it. They whinny in terror.

Will stares as a blur of striped fur and muscle flies out of the cage. The
tribe's totem is a living thing - the saber-toothed tiger ia three times
the size of its Bengal cousin, a head the size of an ox and two ten-inch
teeth curved down either side of its jaw.

Return of the Creatures

The horses are bucking and rearing.
The tiger leaps towards the door,
heading for freedom. A dismounted
ape raises his weapon. The tiger doesn't
even break stride. One lazy swipe
from his paw tears open the armor and
flesh of the ape's chest.

Will can smell the animal's breath
as it flies past. An ape officer, still
on his horse, turns - another swipe
from the tiger's paw rips out his throat.

Kip and his warriors hurl their
spears and stone tomahawks at the cavalry -
half of them dismounted, all of
them in disarray. The tiger runs soars
through the doorway -

OUTSIDE THE CAVE

Drak fights to control his mount as
the tiger lands once and bounds into
the forest.

ON THE LEDGES

Kip's men are fighting as they
retreat, heading towards the
opening at the

roof of the cave. Will, clutching his wounded shoulder, makes his own way
up the wall.

Beneath him, Drak and the apes roll in the third of the machines - a long
iron tube in a rolling superstructure. Feeding it are a series of
oil-filled bladders. One of the apes touches a torch to a firing hole. A
tongue of fire erupts from the end of the tube. It's a flame thrower - The
fiery tongue shoots up towards the roof of the cave. The flame engulfs two
warriors. Skin blazing, they plummet to the ground.

The flame thrower fires again - scorching the rock wall, filling the cave
wit a pall of smoke. It hits the tiny patch of daylight, cutting off escape.

Will - trapped - runs along a ledge, over a pile of rocks and jumps. Into
mid-air! He lands on the back of a riderless horse and drives his heels
into its flanks.

Return of the Creatures

The apes and the surviving warriors turn. For a moment they just stare -
nobody's ever seen a human ride a horse before. Will flies towards the
entrance. He sees Kip on a ledge just above, battling three huge apes.

WILL

Jump!

Kip sees Will galloping towards him. One of the apes raises a double-bladed
sword. Kip jumps sprawling across the horse's neck, grabbing on to its
flowing mane.

Drak stares at Will - he's never seen anything like him. He wheels his
horse around and spurs it forward in pursuit.

OUTSIDE THE CAVE

Will's horse bursts out of the cave - past the Claw and under the Balls.
The apes turn and look - astonished. They scramble for their horses. Drak

Return of the Creatures

charges through.

Will hurtles towards the trees.
Kip, hanging on for life, looks
behind -
Drak raises his Gatling gun and
aims. Kip wrenches Will's head down
- zing!
The arrows skim past.

Drak can't outpace them - and he
can't re-load at the gallop either.
They
charge out of the camp, into -

THE DAPPLED LIGHT OF THE FOREST

Drak rises up in the stirrups and
hauls himself on to the saddlethe
huge
ape stands on the back of the
charging horse!

He jumps - his rippling arms catch
hold of an overhanging bough. He
swings
himself up into the tree - he is an
ape, after all. He throws himself
from
branch to bough, traveling at
incredible speed.

Will glances back - he sees Drak's
riderless horse. His eyes dart in
confusion -where is he? We crane up
- he's in the trees above! Drak
jumps -

Return of the Creatures

Wham! Hundreds of pounds of gorilla blast into Will's shoulder, lifting him
out of the saddle and hurling him to the ground.

Kip hauls down on the horse's bridle - wheeling the stallion around.

Will looks up from the dust - Drak towers above him. Will sees Kip coming
back -

WILL (CONT'D)

Run!

A volley of arrows whiz past Kip - other apes are galloping through the
trees. Kip grabs the bridle and kicks - the horse spins and gallops away.

massive, armor-clad paw grabs Will's head. He looks straight into Drak's
face. The ape reaches out and rips a claw down Will's cheek. Will tries to
stifle the scream. Drak touches the wound and tastes the blood -

DRAK

Return of the Creatures

So - it's human, after ell.

He spits the blood out in revulsion. Will stares into the piu-holes in his
face. Never has he seen eyes so cold.

Will tries to rise to hie feet. His wounded shoulder has weakened him - he
staggers. Drak's clenched fist, clad in chain mail, drives straight et
Will's jaw. Smashl Fade to black.

THE WORLD UPSIDE DOWN

It's Will's point of view - he-s lying on his back in a horse-drawn cart.
He's very weak, his shirt drenched in blood. He rolls over and the image
rights itself.

He drags himself on to all fours but he can't get any further - his legs
are chained.

WILL

(fevered, disoriented)

Where the fuck am I?

Return of the Creatures

Will looks up - a huge ape sits
guard in the back of the wagon.

GUARD

(smiling)

The end of the road.

Will - confused, panicky - grabs
the side of the cart and hauls
himself to
his knees. He looks past an escort
of ape cavalry - they are traveling
down
an avenue of idols -towering
statues of apes, sculpted out of
stone, old as
ages past. Fires burn somewhere
within them giving the eyes a red,
flickering glow.

Will turns away. Behind him he sees
humans, rows of them - dead -
hanging
upsidl down from long poles like
trophies.

Everything comes flooding back - he
slumps against the side of the
cart,
eyes barely focused. Blood trickles
down under his shirt and forms a
pool
between his legs. He doesn't even
notice it.

Return of the Creatures

MASSIVE IRON AND WOOD BRIDGE

spans a roaring river. Drak and his convoy clatter across it. We crane up -
laid out before is a city. Terraces are cut into both sides of a jagged ravine. Opening on to them are caves and houses and buildings made out of
stone.

Apes are everywhere - hammering stones to enlarge a house, chattering in
the trees, swinging hand-over-hand along horizontal ladders - crossing from
one side of the ravine to the other.

Will has roused himself. He stares at the city through feverish eyes - to
him, it appears to float. Buildings swim in and out of focus. His shoulders
shake - he starts to laugh, an edge of hysteria to it.

WILL

A city... of course. Ape city! I've destroyed my mind. Or maybe I'm dead

and this is God's last joke - hell
is ruled by apes.

Whhish - the end of a whip sails
through the air. Crack! It hits
Will's
back, doubling him over.

GUARD

Quiet, animal!

RIPPLES OF WATER

run across the surface of a
beautiful pool. A black shape
glides along
underwater. The head breaks the
surface - it's an old gorilla, the
fur on
his face gray and balding. This is
NAZGUL. He is the Ghan - the
President -
of the Council of Elders.

He walks out of the water. Other
old apes - all male, their days of
warring
and building over - lie around the
pool. Several of them, draped only
in
rough loin-cloths, groom each
other, picking nits out of their
fur.

Return of the Creatures

The sound of a gong! Nazgul picks up a loin cloth and walks the end of the
pool. He looks straight down the ravine - at the far end, Drak and his
troop come into view.

NAZGUL

The raiders are home.

OLD APE

(lazily)

Good hunting?

Nazgul squints against the sun. He sees the poles carrying the dead humans.

NAZGUL

By the look of it.

GRAY-BEARDED WARRIOR, HIS CHEST MARKED BY THE SCARS OF MANY BATTLES, GETS
UP -

GRAY BEARD

(proudly)

Not as good as when we rode the high ridges, I'll warrant.

Return of the Creatures

NAZGUL

Times are different now. Back then, a could go out and come back with a brace of animals. They're far scarcer now -

OLD APE

Not scarce enough, I say.

There's a murmur of agreement from the other apes.

A TINY BOAT

is wreathed in woven leaves. Lying in it is the dead body of a young ape.
The boat drifts down an underground stream. All around it rise the stone
walls of a huge cavern. Torches light up the gloom - this place is a
temple.

A group of apes - mourners - walk along a path, keeping pace with the funeral boat.

They make a humming sound deep in the back of their throats - a dirge for
the dead.

Return of the Creatures

At the head of the procession,
swinging a smoking censer, is an
ape wearing
a lion-skin cloak. His face is
scarred and twisted - he has one
cruel eye,
the other is just an empty socket.
Beneath the cloak, one arm and a
leg are
withered. The whole effect, rather
than diminishing his power,
enhances it.
His name is MA-GOG. He is high
priest of the apes, defender of the
faith,
keeper of the Book of the Lore.

The funeral boat gathers speed in
the current. It thrusts towards
sunlight
pouring through an arch.

A ROCK PLATFORM

The mourners step through the arch
and on to a slab of rock. We pull
back
to reveal where they stand - a huge
crouching ape has been carved out
of
the face of a cliff, Its bowed
front legs form the archway, the
entrance to
the temple of the ape.

Return of the Creatures

CLOUDS OF MIST AND WIND-BLOWN SPRAY SWEEP OVER MA-GOG AND THE MOURNERS. ALL
AROUND THEM, THE SOUND OF ROARING WATER. THE FUNERAL BOAT FLOATS OUT OF THE
TEMPLE AND INTO A ROARING RIVER. MA-GOG SWINGS THE CENSER OVER THE WATER -

MA -GOG

(intoning)

In the beginning was the word, and the word was the Book of the Lore. It
says God created the ape in His own image. Alone among His creatures, the
ape has a soul. One crosses the river now but death is only a door. He will
dwell in the house of the Lord forever. Amen The mourners beat their chests
with their fists. They repeat the word "Amen".

For a moment the clouds of mist clear. Now we see where the boat is headed
- half an ocean of water pours over a sheer drop. These are the Falls of No
Return. The boat races forward - over the waterfall it goes.

Return of the Creatures

The sound of cheering voices, very faint, drifts towards them. Ma-Gog turns
and looks up the river towards the city -

APES HANG FROM THE 'LADDERS'

looking down on Drak and his troops. The convoy passes along a road cut
into the side of the ridge. Apes have come out of the houses and buildings
to greet them.

Will lies in the back of the cart, unconscious. Faces of apes stare in at
him - they've never seen anything like it. A young ape - a little boy -
stands with his grandfather.

KID

What is it?

GRANDFATHER

Some... sort of human.

KID

But look at the eyes, 'Pa - they're
the color of the sea. Where's it
from?

GRANDFATHER

I don't know - a traveler, maybe.
Nobody knows what lies beyond the
Tower
of the Moon.

THE WORD "TRAVELER" IS PICKED UP BY
OTHER APES. IT RIPPLES THROUGH THE
CROWD. A WOMAN ON THE OTHER SIDE OF
THE WAGON CALLS OUT -

WOMAN

No it's not - it's a mutant.

LABORER

Put it in the zoo!

A female ape pushes them aside.
She's heavy-set, bright eyes, an
air of
authority about her. Over her
shoulder she carries a leather
satchel with a
series of steel instruments
dangling from it. Her name is ZORA
- she is a
doctor.

Return of the Creatures

She and her ASSISTANT - a young male - swing themselves on to the cart.
Kneeling beside him, Zora puts her hand down and grabs hold of Will's crotch.

ZORA

Whatever it is, it's male.

She rips open Will's shirt - his chest is covered in blood from the gaping
wound.

ZORA (CONT'D)

Probe.

The Assistant hands her a steel instrument. She slides it towards the
wound. We hold on Will's face - a strangled cry but he doesn't regain consciousness. Zore returns the bloodied probe to her Assistant. She calls
out -

ZORA (CONT'D)

Drak!

The leader of the ape warriors, riding close by, turns -

ZORA (CONT'D)

The animal's bleeding to death, my Lord.

Drak rides up to the wagon.

DRAK

I didn't bring him all this way just to have him die.

ZORA

(to the assistant)

Ben-Guri - get a vet. Quicklyl

AN APE IN A LEATHER APRON

uses a grinding wheel to sharpen a gruesome looking knife. This is the VET.
Will lies on a stone slab nearby - it's a sort of medical centersinks along
the walls, racks of equipment, hoses to wash down the blood.

The Vet cuts the clothing away from Will's wound. He turns to Doctor Zora -

VET

We're going to have to give him blood.

Return of the Creatures

```
PRISONER IN A CELL

He's a tribesman - in his late 40s.
Despite his tattered furs and hollow
cheeks, he carries himself with
dignity - he's a proud man. His name is
ARAGORN. On a chain around his neck
he wears a metal ornament, like
crescent moon. Etched into it are
strange markings and the totems of
various tribes.

The sound of a key in lock. Aragorn
turns - the cell door is thrown back.
Three ape guards enter. Two of
them, armed with spears, drive
Aragorn into
a corner. The third ape has a
leather collar on the end of a
pole. He drops
it over Aragorn's head.

Aragorn struggles but the ape jerks
the collar tight. They drag him from
the cell.

TEAM OF HORSES

- their flanks drenched in sweat -
walk in a circle. They turn a huge
wheel
```

that controls a series of pulleys and winches. Attached to the end of a
heavy cable is a wooden platform - a primitive elevator. It runs from a
series of impressive house, down the side of the ravine, to the center of
the city.

Standing on the platform are Nazgul and several other elders. They look down on the central square. It's crowded with apes - soldiers are being
greeted by their kin.

ARAGORN LIES ON HIS BACK

He's strapped to a slab, half-naked, in the medical center. They've put a
gag in his mouth and though he struggles to free himself, he can barely
move.

Will, still unconscious, lies on a table next to him. Nazgul peers down at
him.

NAZGUL

It's human, you say?

Return of the Creatures

Doctor Zora nods - yes.

NAZGUL

It's even uglier than the others.

He pulls a covering aside and looks at Will's naked legs.

NAZGUL (CONT'D)

How can he hunt with legs like those -they're like twigs. Maybe he's
diseased.

Everybody shrugs - who knows?

The Vet heats a steel needle over an open flame. The other end of the needle is attached to a length of animal intestine. It acts as a tube. The
Vet grabs Will's forearm and slides the red-hot needle into the vein. Will's body jerks with the pain. Nazgul and the others spring back.

For a moment Will's wrenched back to consciousness - he sees a light-filled
room, a bandage on his chest, a bladder full of blood hanging above him.
His puts it together the only way he knows - he thinks he's in hospital

Return of the Creatures

WILL

(groggy)

Help me. I've got health insurance. Honest...

His eyes close as he slips back into darkness. Nazgul looks at Doctor Zora.

NAZGUL

What is health insurance?

DOCTOR ZORA

Some sort of religion...?

The Vet turns and makes an adjustment to the bladder. Another length of
tubing snakes out of it and is attached by a needle to Aragorn's arm. It's
his blood. Now we realize - this is the ape version of a blood transfusion.

NAZGUL

Do you think this'll work?

VET

Return of the Creatures

You can never tell with animals.
Their bodies aren't as
sophisticated as an
ape's. Sometimes their blood fights
with each other. Either way, you know
really quick -they get up and walk
around, or they're dead.

The Vet turns a little tap -
Aragorn's blood flows down the
tube. It hits
Will's vein.

WORDS CHISELED INTO STONE

"An Ape without knowledge is a fire
without light."

Euripadape III

It stands over the doorway of a
building high on a ridge. This is
the Hall
of Learning. Ma-Gog - his lion skin
cloak billowing behind him -
hurries up
the steps.

THE BLADDER OF BLOOD

is empty. Guards are collaring
Aragorn, preparing to drag him out.
The door
into the room is thrown open. Ma-
Gog enters. Nazgul and the others
greet

him but he barely acknowledges it *

MA-GOG

Show him to me.

The Vet grabs Will's hair. He lifts up his head so that Ma-Gog can see his
face.

The high priest takes a step back - there's something about Will that fills
him with loathing. Anger flashes in his one good eye. He stares at Will.
His voice is low, almost to himself -

MA-GOG (CONT'D)

All my life I've dreaded this day.

(turns to the others)

Kill him.

DOCTOR ZORA

We've just spent an hour trying to save him -

MA-GOG

Kill him!

Return of the Creatures

He grabs the stand holding the bladder and throws it to the ground. Doctor
Zora takes his arm, stopping him -

DOCTOR ZORA

The animal's unique, my lord. At least we should look at his brain. Maybe
it's possible to remove the frontal lobes without killing him. Imagine - a
tame human!

MA-GOG

Man can't be tamed. Alone among God's primates he kills for lust or greed.
He will murder his own brother to possess his brother's land.

NAZGUL

The doctor's only asking for a chance to experiment. The benefits would be
enormous. A tame species of human could double food production, at last we
could dam the rivers.

MA-GOG

You don't know what you're dealing with.

Return of the Creatures

NAZGUL

It's just an animal, Ma-Gog.

MA-GOG

It's not. That's the trouble.

A movement on the stone slab. They turn and look - Will's eyelids are fluttering. He's starting to come round. itl

He turns to Nazgul In the name of God - summon the Council of Elders.

Will's eyes are open now. Like through a glass - darkly - he sees the ape
guards coming for him. He tries to struggle but he's very weak. They haul
him off.

HEAVY IRON DOOR

set in a rock wall - on one side a key-hole. We tilt up the door to a narrow set of bars high above it. A face, straining with effort, rises up
to peer through the bars. It is Will - looking like death but forcing
himself to do it, desperate to see where he is.

Return of the Creatures

INSIDE THE CELL

The muscles across his shoulders ripple. His one good hand clutches the
bars. He hangs by it, supporting his weight, staring out at a vaulted
underground cavern. It looks like a cattle-yard, broken down and disused
nowa series of long pens, wooden chutes and a primitive conveyor belt.

Will can't support himself any longer - he tumbles to the ground. He crawls
across the floor and examines the door. It fits tight to the rock. There's
no hope of picking the lock - the key-hole doesn't even come all the way
through.

Suddenly he stops. Nothing for a moment, then he hears it again - a scraping sound.

He peers under the wooden bed at the stone blocks that form wall. One of
the blocks moves. Will grabs hold of it and hauls it into the cell. Aragorn

squeezes through from the adjoining cell. He looks at Will -

ARAGORN

So you lived, then?

WILL

What did they do?

ARAGORN

They gave you blood.

He holds up his bandaged forearm - Will realizes where it came from.

WILL

I hope you had a medical.

Aragorn looks at him - confused. From a distance, the sound of horses
whinnying.

WILL (CONT'D)

What is this place?

ARAGORN

It was a slaughterhouse.

WILL

Return of the Creatures

For horses?

ARAGORN

They use it for stables now. No - s different kind of animal. For humans.

Will stares, taken aback. Aragorn starts to gather twigs from the corners
of the cell.

ARAGORN (CONT'D)

In my father's time, the apes rounded up tribes and brought them here.
Young apes killed some during their manhood rites, the others were made sport of in the corrals. At the end, the bodies were thrown onto the belts
and fed to the fire.

Aragorn has made a pyramid of twigs and leaves. From out of his cloak, he
takes two pieces of flint and strikes them. A spark starts the fire -

ARAGORN (CONT'D)

(softly)

Return of the Creatures

Death is stuck to these walls,
stranger -sounds not even s
thousand winters
can take away. Sometimes of s night
they speak to me - I can hear the
screams of my people.

Will looks at him. Firelight plays
across their faces.

WILL

Why haven't they killed you?

ARAGORN

They keep me ss bait. My name is
Aragorn -

He lifts his hand to Will - palm
outwards. It's some form of
greeting. Will
returns it.

ARAGORN (CONT'D)

I am the Ranger of the Easterlings,
the Leader of the Seven Tribes.
They
hope the warriors will come and try
to free me.

WILL

And will they?

ARAGORN

Return of the Creatures

Not if they fear my anger. I was taken in summer and now winter's almost
gone. Even the apes grow tired - soon they'll make me walk the Paths of the
Dead.

Will looks at Aragorn's eyes - they're fearless. The ornament glints on his
chest. Will points at it -

WILL

what is it?

ARAGORN

It's called the Crescent of Light - it's the talisman of my rank.

WILL

Silver.

ARAGORN

Mithral is how we name it..

Will reaches his hand towards it -

WILL

Can I borrow it?

Return of the Creatures

Aragorn recoils - this is the most
precious thing in the world to him.
His
hand closes around the insignia -

ARAGORN

Who are you? What brings you to the
valley of the tribes?

WILL

I meant you no harm. I'm looking
for woman, one of my own kind. Do
you know
of people like me?

ARAGORN

Never.

Will nods his head, accepting it.
Slowly he reaches his hand out -

WILL

If you want to get out of hare. I
need the talisman. Aragorn.

The two men look at each other. A
beat - then Aragorn reaches up and
unfastens it.

THE TEMPLE OF THE APE

Torches burn on the walls. They
cast a glow across the temple - the

underground stream, pools of water, shelves of rock hewn out of the walls.
Several apes crouch on them, praying to a golden idol of an ape.

Mist rises off of the pools. Moving through it, we see Nazgul, Drak and e
group of old apes. The Council of Elders is gathering. They pass through a
narrow door -

THE TEMPLE'S INNER CHAMBER

Oil lamps - hidden in alcoves - illuminate Ma-Gog. He stands in front of an
ancient book - strange symbols, like Sanskrit, run across its pages. This
is the Book of the Lore.

Ma-Gog looks at the Council of Elders seated in front of himNazgul, Drak
and five other huge apes - all leaders in their time.

MA-GOG

How many scrolls are there in the Book of the Lore?

Nobody replies - the question is so obvious it needs no answer.

Return of the Creatures

MA-GOG (CONT'D)

One-hundred-and-seventy-six, you say -every child knows that.

(softly)

But every child is wrong. There is one more scroll - the last scroll, sealed with seven seals, handed down from high priest to high priest...

He slides his hand under the top of the pedestal and releases a hidden catch. The top - the Book still resting on it - tilts up, revealing a
secret compartment. It is lined with gold leaf. Lying in it is a slim folio
of pages -

MA-GOG (CONT'D)

It is called the Scroll of Revelation.

The Council of Elders stare in awed silence. Ma-Gog takes the pages out and
unfastens the seals. He reads -

MA-GOG (CONT'D)

Return of the Creatures

"And it was given unto me to know the wisdom of ages. A silence fell and I
saw a new heaven and a new earth. Like through a glass, darkly, I saw the
future."

The Council of Elders stare at him. He limps forward and stops in front of
them. He recites from memory -

MA-GOG (CONT'D)

"Behold - there rose out of the earth a pale horse and the name of the
horse is Death. Those that ride on him are beasts, but like no beasts born
before. Their limbs are weak but their eyes are as cold as the sea. They
are given power over the earth to kill with the sword and with famine and
with fire. And let him that hath understanding know the number of these
beasts. It is the number of Man."

He raises his eyes and looks straight at the Councilors.

MA-GOG (CONT'D)

Return of the Creatures

Today we saw that beast. Mark those words, my Lords - "their limbs are weak
but they are given power over the earth". Now will you listen? Kill him!
And if we don't? Then all hope will fail in this bitter winter.

He lays down the secret scroll and closes the secret compartment. Nazgul
looks from one to the other of the elders. Nobody says a word but he can
read their grim expressions. He turns to Drek -

NAZGUL

Kill him. Kill him with the sword and with fire. Kill himl

THE KEYHOLE TO THE CELL

It's a shining bright image, slightly distorted. We pull back to reveal
it's a reflection. Aragorn's silver ornament has been polished to a brilliant luster. It's fixed to the end of a length of wood sticking through the bars high above the iron door.

INSIDE THE CELL

Return of the Creatures

The wooden bed has been smashed to pieces.

Both Aragorn and Will have used parts of their clothing to harness themselves so they can see through the bars. Aragorn controls the pole with
the "mirror" on the end of it.

By looking into it, Will can see the keyhole on the other side of the door.
He has a pole with a nail attached to the end of it. He turns the pole,
guiding the nail towards the keyhole. He's trying to pick the lock.

WILL

Do you understand time.., what time is it?

Aragorn looks at the shadows in the slaughterhouse -

ARAGORN

Seven hours since the rising of the sun.

WILL

Just after noon...

Return of the Creatures

ARAGORN

Shouldn't we wait until night?

WILL

(concentrating)

If I'm right, it's gonna be dark a lot sooner than you think.

The nail is almost in the key-hole. Half an inch to go... a quarter. It slides off. Will curses and starts again -

THE SUN

beats down from a cloudleu sky. Drak and two huge Praetorian Guards - Max
and Hannibal - come through a huge stone portico. It's another entrance to
the Temple -one that opertl onto a central square. Orak and the two guards
hurry across it. towards the slaughterhouu.

THE NAIL

at the end of the pole slides into the keyhole. Will - barely breathing in

case it breaks his concentration - listens carefully. He moves the end of
the pole. The nail turns.

HUGE SET OF DOORS

are thrown open. Daylight spills into the slaughterhouse. Drak, Max and
Hannibal enter. Drak stops - he listens to the horses whinnying and stomping their hooves -

DRAK

Something's wrong!

(turns to Max)

Get the dogs.

HANNIBAL

moves cautiously along the side one of the corrals, trying to see what's
wrong with the horses. Behind him - a movement in the shadows.

Sswhish. The sound of something slicing through the air. He turns -

It's the side of Aragorn's hand. It chops hard into the ape's throat,

shattering his larynx and blasting him into unconsciousness. He crumples to
the ground.

Aragorn and Will strip him of his weapons. Will starts to go but Aragorn
tears a strip off both their shirts. He ties the fabric around the ape's
ankles.

WILL

What are you doing?

ARAGORN

Watch - they're going to bring in the dogs.

THE DOGS

aren't really dogs at all - they're a much earlier ancestor. We call them
wolves. There are two of them, on the end of heavy leather leashes. Their
handlers have them in Will's cell, rubbing parts of the abandoned harnesses
in front of their noses. The wolves take the scent.

Return of the Creatures

Drak watches as the handlers
unfasten the leashes. The wolves
leap out of
the cell.

HANNIBAL

rises groggily to his feet,
clutching his injured throat. He
takes a few
steps forward -Grrrr! He turns -
the two wolves fly towards him. He
tries
to yell but the only sound he can
make is a squeak.

He runs - the fabric, unseen by
him, trails from his ankles. The
wolves
pound after him. He glances over
his shoulder. First one wolf - then
the
other - leaps.

Fangs and claws glistening, they
hit him in the back, hurling him to
the
ground. He writhes on to his back.
One wolf tears at his ankles, the
other
goes for his throat. Rip! Blood
sprays as the artery breaks.

A STONE PASSAGE-WAY

Return of the Creatures

Will and Aragorn are running,
plunging down in to darkness.
Arches and
corridors open off of it. It's like
a labyrinth -

WILL

This doesn't seem like the way out.

ARAGORN

We're not going out - not yet.

WILL STOPS, GRABBING HOLD OF HIM,
TURNING HIM ROUND -

WILL

So what are we doing?

ARAGORN

(softly)

We're going killing.

WILL

Killing?! Don't be stupid -

Will jerks on Aragorn's arm,
starting to haul him back. Aragorn
throws off
his hand -

ARAGORN

Return of the Creatures

You do what you like! But I'm the
Ranger of the Easterlings -I won't leave
here until it's done.

From behind them - the sounds of pursuit.

WILL

Shit!

He starts to run. Together they
disappear into the gloom ahead.

ROW OF CAGE-LIKE CELLS

Will and Aragorn glide past them.
They're taking it slowly, very
carefully.

Now we see why - ahead of them is a
set of steel doors. Torches on either
side illuminate a guard post but
there's no sign of the sentry.

Will and Aragorn move closer. They
pass -

CREVICE IN THE ROCK

We hold on the narrow opening,
looking deep into the shadows. A
big ape,

Return of the Creatures

heavily armed, stands there. He has his back to us, his legs spread. A trickle of water runs down the rock and drains away - he's taking a piss. A
shadow flickers on the wall above him. He sees it -THE PASSAGE-WAYMore
shadows -Will and Aragorn are move through the torchlight. The steel doors
are straight ahead.

The sentry slides out of the crevice - he's behind Will. Silently, back
pressed again6t the bars of a cell, he creeps closer to Will. He has a curved knife in one hand and a short-handled spear in the other. Closer...
closer.

He raises the spear - a rustle of movement. Will spins - he sees the spear
about to thrust. He's a dead man.

An arm? It shoots between the bars of the cell and locks around the sentry's throat, half choking him.

Will leaps forward and drives the butt of a weapon into the sentry's jaw.

111

Return of the Creatures

The sentry crumples to the ground,
revealing the face of the prisoner. It's
not a man, though -it's an ape.
He's in his prime - barrel chested and a
fine head. His name is STRIDER.

He and Will look at each other
through the bars.

STRIDER

Two rules in life - never play
cards with anyone called Doc and never,
whatever else you do, turn your
back on an ape.

Will stares at him. Strider grins.
Will smiles back -

WILL

Thanks. I'll remember that.

He starts to search the sentry.

ARAGORN

What are you doing?

WILL

Looking for the keys.

ARAGORN

No!

WILL

He saved our lives.

ARAGORN

He's an ape!

Will shrugs himself free of Aragorn's hand -

WILL

You go and kill as many apes as you like - I'm setting this one free.

Aragorn looks at him. A beat.

ARAGORN

(softly)

It's not apes I'm going to kill.

A PRISON LABORATORY

The heavy steel doors stand open. Inside is a clean and gruesome room -
sinks and instruments along a wall, a series of operating tables and a row
of cages.

Return of the Creatures

Behind the bars are six tribes-people - men, women and a little boy. All of them carry surgical scars on their heads. It's made two of them blind; the others stare blankly into space.

Aragorn moves down the cages. Several of them shuffle towards him but there's no recognition - they're like the walking dead. Aragorn doesn't say a word. Grim-faced, he loads the crossbow and starts to fire, killing them.

Will and Strider come through the doorway - they see Aragorn going from cage to cage. Will steps forward, going to stop him. Strider's hand grabs his shoulder, restraining him.

STRIDER

Leave it. He knows what he's doing.

Will turns and looks at him, questioning.

STRIDER (CONT'D)

The doctors operate on them - up here.

Return of the Creatures

(taps his head)

The tribes think that we steal their souls...

(he pauses - softly)

Maybe they're right.

Aragorn reaches the last cage. A woman - in her 20s - stands in the middle
of the cell, looking at him. Aragorn stares at her face. His lip trembles
with emotion. She tilts her head on one side, as if trying to work
something out. Tears fill Aragorn's eyes. She stumbles a step forward. The
Ranger closes his eyes. He pulls the trigger. A crossbow bolt slams into
her chest and she falls.

Will leans against the doorway, unwilling to watch, staring down the
passageway. He turns at a footfall - Aragorn rejoins them. His voice is
hollow, as if something has died within him -

ARAGORN

Return of the Creatures

It's done. We can go now.

He turns and leads them back down the passageway.

THE WOLVES

There's five of them now, hunting through the slaughter-house in a pack.
All around them we see the torches of the apes as they search the nooks and
crannies. The horses whinny wildly as they catch the scent of the wolves.

Will, Aragorn and Strider are crouched in a corner of the corral, smearing
their bodies with horse manure.

STRIDER

The fresher the better. Cover everything -that's the only way you'll hide
your scent.

The wolves sniff the air, coming closer. Will, staring through the rungs of
the coral, sees their gleaming eyes coming closer. He raises his crossbow,
getting ready.

Return of the Creatures

The wolves stop. They raise their heads and look - the whole cavern is
growing dark. A giant shadow falls across the doorway into the outside world.

The horses rear and buck. The apes are staring - darkness is falling in the
middle of the day. The wolves hackles rise in fear. They howl.

Aragorn and Strider are cowering back

ARAGORN

What is it?

WILL

Come on! Now!

He drags them forward and grabs hold of one of the horses.

AN UNEARTHLY LIGHT

has fallen on the city. The apes are in confusion - soldiers and workers
are running, children are screaming. A horse has thrown its rider and is
bolting down the terraces.

Return of the Creatures

The darkness grows ever deeper. In the sky, the face of the moon obliterates the sun - it's a full solar eclipse.

Two horses, flying at a gallop, charge through the doors of the slaughterhouse. Will is on one, Aragorn clinging to his back. Strider is on
the other. They wheel across an open space, through running apes, and speed
down a terrace.

MA-GOG

steps out on to a rock ledge. He holds a staff in one hand, his cloak
thrown back over his shoulder, magnificent in the eerie light. He stares
down at the chaos. Drak swings across a ladder and lands at his side -

DRAK

What is it?

MA-GOG

(wild)

Return of the Creatures

A sign - the hand of Man passes
across the face of God! Lookl He
points to
a terrace below - Will leads the
other two escapees along a road and
on to
the iron bridge. Drak and Ma-Gog
stare at them. Darkness engulfs
them.

Out of the blackness, an image -

CHRIST ON THE CROSS

It's a stained-glass window in a
huge cathedral. A priest is at the
altar
conducting Mass for the repose of
the dead. We pull back to reveal a
tiny
white coffin - just big enough for
a baby. Next to it is another
coffin.
And another - a row of them.

PRIEST

And even now as sorrow has no end,
we find comfort in the words of the
Lord
Jesus Christ. Did he not say unto
Mark -"suffer the little children
to come
unto me, for they are the Kingdom
of Heaven. Now and forever." Amen.

Return of the Creatures

The congregation - sad-eyed relatives and weeping parents - fill the pews.

CONGREGATION

Amen.

Pall-bearers lift up the tiny coffins. The organ starts to play. A soloist
- a tenor -steps to the side of the altar. He starts to sing the Latin hymn
"Penis Angelicas". The haunting words of the hymn fill the cathedral. They
carry over to -

THE SPACE DOME

is lit up by banks of lights that turn night into day. The clock tower
above the biology building shows the time2.00am. Even so, the area bustles
with activity.

INSIDE THE DOME

An illuminated chart dominates one wall - just like the strategy map in the
Pentagon's war room. Every research center is identified - next to it is

Return of the Creatures

its function and a list of
personnel. We see Princeton,
Stanford, Texas
A&M, Los Alamos. Tentacles reach
out to Oxford, the Pasteur
Institute, the
University of Beijing...

Below the chart are nitrogen-cooled
Cray super-computers. We track
through
teams of men and women processing
data, satellite dishes feeding a
communications network, a video
conference taking place in a
corner,
technicians routing and re-routing
phone calls and faxes.

We come to a glass wall. On the
other side is Diamond -

A SMALL OFFICE

Glass doors seal out the electronic
hum. Diamond, staring through the
glass, looks exhausted.
DeMaupassent sits on a couch. He's
in his
shirt-sleeves, dark rings under his
eyes. Next to him is Bob, the young
neurologist. He wears jeans and a
t-shirt. On the front it says

"I'll sleep when I'm dead."

Return of the Creatures

The coffee table is piled with files, journal extracts and computer
print-outs. A video projector beams a complex molecular structure on to a
screen.

Diamond rubs her eyes, trying to wipe away the fatigue.

DIAMOND

I'm sorry Luc - say that again.

DEMAUPASSANT

DEMAUPASSANT (CONT'D)

(kindly)

My fault, Billie - I rattle on too much. The result is - we've fixed the
time frame.

He hits the projector - the image of a fetus developing normally in the
womb appears on the screen...
deMAUPASSANT

The fetus develops normally through the first trimester. Then it happens -
about sixteen weeks and two days, everything falls apart. The whole

chemical structure goes out of control –

He flashes up another image – a fetus that is already aging remarkably.

deMAUPASSANT

Once it starts, it's irreversible. If we're going to stop it, we've got to
intercede here –

He points at the slide of the normally developing fetus.

BOB

(taking over)

There's a trigger – some major fucking switch gets turned. That's what I've
been working on. It's definitely in the mDNA. There's a fragment of one chromosome I'm looking at –

He flicks a switch on the video projector. A slide of a human gene, massively magnified, popl on to the screen.

BOB (CONT'D)

It's so different, I call it the alien. How it got there, exactly what it does - I haven't got the first idea.., no fucking idea at all.

Diamond looks at his grim face. He seems totally defeated.

DIAMOND

(quietly)

Is it that bad?

He stares at the floor. There's not even a hint of the former arrogance.

BOB

Someone's dropped us in the middle of the Louvre. We're blind men and they've told us to find the Mona Lisa. There's four miles of galleries end
we've got five minutes to do it. That's how I feel -and that's when rm
optimistic.

Diamond turns to deMaupassant.

DIAMOND

Luc?

DEMAUPASSANT

Return of the Creatures

I'm sixty-two years old. I've seen us go from DC3s to landing on the moon.
In my life I've won all the glittering prizes. I've always believed nothing
was beyond the reach of Man, but I'll tell you honestly - this may never be
unraveled. If it is, it won't be in my lifetime.

He looks at them. Silence. There's nothing anyone can say. He starts to
gather up his papers-

DEMAUPASSANT (CONT'D)

So what do we do? I think it's like Gatsby -"so we beat on, boats against
the current, borne back ceaselessly into the past." There's no other way,
ia there?

They nod their hoods - you have to try. DeMaupaasant and Bob start to leave.

DIAMOND

Luc?

(he turns))

You're certain - about the time, I
mean?

DEMAUPASSANT

(Nodding)

Sixteen weeks. How far along are
you?

DIAMOND

Twelve weeks.

They look at one another. The old
man speaks gently -

DEMAUPASSANT

Good night, Billie.

A TINY FETUS

perfectly formed - floats in the
amniotic fluid. It's alive - the
large
head sways, the heart beats through
the translucent ribs.

Diamond has her shirt pulled up and
her jeans down around her thighs.
She
lies on a stainless steel table in
a hi-tach examination room. A
complex

array of equipment -ultra-sounds
and scanners - beams down on her exposed
stomach. It projects a , video
image onto a screen.

She is alone in the room,
manipulating the equipment herself.
She stares up
at the child growing in her womb.
We see the genitalia.

DIAMOND

So - you're a little boy. It's
funny - I think I knew.

She reaches up and gently touches
the image of his face.

DIAMOND (CONT'D)

We've got four weeks. The way I see
it -there's nothing to lose. I can't
tell you whet'll happen to us. It's
on the edge, mister. The air's so thin
out there, we may not even be able
to breathe. But what the hell -
it's a
chance.

She takes her hand away and looks
at his face.

DIAMOND (CONT'D)

Return of the Creatures

You want to try it? Sure you do.
You're my son. We've waited all our lives
for each other.

A STACK OF HAND-WRITTEN NOTEPADS

lie on a table in the basement. We
track through them - past computer
print-outs and dog-eared journals.
We recognize them - these are Will's
detailed notes.

To the table is the makeshift lab -
racks of bottles and syringes. In the
dim light we see Diamond. She
removes the catheter from her vein, turns and
climbs up the flotation tank.

INSIDE THE TANK

Water sloshes back and forth.
Diamond lowers herself in and
floats there.
For a moment, she stares up at the
circle of light spilling through the
hatch. We hold on her face.

DIAMOND (CONT'D)

(softly)

Return of the Creatures

So we beat on, boats against the current.

She reaches up and pulls the hatch shut. Clang! Darkness.

THE SUN AND THE MOON

It's one of those strange twilights when both celestial bodies hang in the
sky together. Smoke drifts across them. We tilt down to ape city -

A column of smoke and flame spirals out of a stone chimney on top of the
slaughterhouse.

RED HOT FIRE

burns in a huge furnace at one end of the slaughterhouse. The rickety conveyor belt is working, clattering away. Several ape workers throw the
bodies of the lab animals - the dead tribes-people - on to the belt.

The body of the young boy is carried forward on the belt. It dumps him into
the furnace. The flames engulf him.

WILL'S EMPTY CELL

Return of the Creatures

The door hangs open. The space is lit by a dozen torches. Drak is alone,
moving around the cell, trying to work out how Will escaped. He looks at
the smashed bed, the hole in the wall, the torn clothing that made the
harness.

He swings the heavy door on its hinges and touches the lock. No answers
there. Lying in the doorway is the length of wood with the nail in the end.
Drak picks it up. He turns it over in his hand, th!nking about it.

He jumps! One handed he catches hold of the bars above the door.
Effortlessly, he hauls himself up and pokes the wood through the bars. The
nail touches the lock.

DRAK

(to himself)

Clever... you clever fucking animal.

DOCTOR ZORA (O.S.)

My lord...

He turns and sees the doctor hurrying towards him.

DOCTOR ZORA (CONT'D)

(urgent)

Could I see you please?

THE HALL OF POWER

is a magnificent room - stone columns and towering trees growing in huge
pots. At one end is a rock shelf - open to the gathering twilight. Silhouetted against it, commanding a view of the entire city, is the Council of Elders. They sit around a table made from bone and tusks, deep
in discussion.

Nazgul looks up - he sees Drak approaching through the shadows.

NAZGUL

Drak. I was just saying - maybe it's a blessing.

DRAK

A blessing?

NAZGUL

Return of the Creatures

Where there's one, there must be
others. If we'd killed him, we
might never
find them.

MA-GOG

But the animal's not stupid - he
knows come day-break we'll be
tracking
him. Who's to say he'll run for
home?

Drak stops in front of them.

DRAK

No - he's not stupid. But even dogs
hunt in packs of seven. Every
animal
needs its kind. And when we find
them - what then?

MA-GOG

What do you think?!

DRAK

Just like the tribes - burn them
out of their holes, put them to the
sword?
I don't mind doing that - I like it
- but it's never enough, is it? No

matter how many we kill, every year they're still here. Why will it be any
different with the Blue Eyes? What we need is a final solution.

NAZGUL And where do we find that?

DRAK (CONT'D)

Doctor Zora's brought back patients from a place called Kismatu. I've been
talking to her about it -

Several of the Council are looking at each other - perplexed.

MA-GOG

What is Kismatu?

NAZGUL

It's a tiny colony farther out than even the northern frontier. Females and
babies have been dying there.

He turns to Drak - his eyes intense, very interested.

NAZGUL (CONT'D)

Go on.

COOL AND LOVELY ROOM

Return of the Creatures

There are iron barn on I series of high windows but in the middle of the
room is a jungle-gym. Underneath it are ape toys. Five baby apes sit on cots. They must be no more than two or three years old but their faces end
bodies are those of old, old apeswizened and wrinkled, frail with age.

A double set of bars provide a sort of air-lock. Hanging on them is a sign

"Quarantine. No Entry".

Drak and the Council of Elders stare in at the children. Doctor Zora is
with them - she's nervous, twisting her fingers.

DOCTOR ZORA

We don't know what causes it- a virus probably. I'd hoped to complete our
research before I came to you with my proposal. But, given the circumstances -

NAZGUL I

It's a brilliant idea.

Return of the Creatures

(turns and smiles at her)

Brilliant.

HORSES' HOOVES

paw the ground. They're bound with cloth to stop them leaving a trail. It's
night -the horses are tethered near a fire burning in the lee of a rock.

Will and Strider have made camp - a hare roasts over the fire. Aragorn sits
well apart - a silhouette in the moonlight - staring out into the forest,
lost in his thoughts. Will and Strider look at him.

STRIDER

He's their leader - he can never take his eye from the mountain. He has to
do what he thinks is right.

WILL

(hard)

By killing them?

STRIDER

Don't judge him, Will. I couldn't have done it. I wonder if you could? One
of those women he just killed wes his daughter.

Will reacts. He turns and stares at the silhouette. A long beat.

WILL

(quietly)

We call it a Iobotomy. What other things have you people tried?

He turns to face him. Strider shrugs. There's something about it -

something almost evasive.

WILL (CONT'D)

Fuck you, Strider! Tell me!

He stares at Will - he's never seen him angry.

STRIDER

don't know if it's true.., my sister's mate works in the lab. He says
Doctor Zora's working on some disease -

Return of the Creatures

Will comes towards him –

WILL

What sort of disease?

STRIDER

Of the children, I think – ape children.

WILL

How did they die, Strider? Old in the belly –is that how?!

STRIDER

Some of them. You know this disease?

Will stares at him, taking it in.

WILL

(softly)

So that's how it happened. Fuck you people.

STRIDER

They haven't done it yet. It may not work.

WILL

They will and it does.

He turns end takes step towards the forest. He runs his fingers through his
hair -WILL God help us.

STRIDER

That's funny - that's exactly what an ape would say.

Will turns. He and Strider stare at one another - the ape and the man, both
struck by the sudden commonality.

STRIDER (CONT'D)

I'm sorry...

Will walks slowly back to the fire. Strider starts to strip the meat off a
hare he's roasting over the flames. He offers it to Will. He shakes his head - he's not hungry anymore. He stares into the flames -

WILL

What about you, Strider - why were you in the cell?

STRIDER

Return of the Creatures

I fought another ape. Nothing very
heroic, I'm afraid - I was drunk.
He
fell badly, his head hit the branch
of a tree going down. It broke his
neck.

He pauses We're not like humans. An
ape never kills one of his own.
Never.

WILL

What's the punishment?

STRIDER

At the ceremony of summer rites,
the high priest would curse me with
death.

I would have been left to die in
the forest -no journey over the
waterfall,
no-one to say the sacred words.
Without that, no ape can walk in
the next
world. You saved my life, Will and
I'm grateful. But there's nothing I
can
do about my soul. I'm a dead ape
walking.

Strider stripe more meet off the
hare. Will picks up a saddle and
blanket
and starts to make himself bed.

STRIDER (CONT'D)

You knew, didn't you? You knew the sun was going to swallow the moon. That's why you weren't afraid.

Will pauses - then he turns to him.

WILL

Yes - I knew.

STRIDER

WHO ARE YOU, WILL?

WILL

I've come a long way, Strider - it's farther then I can explain.

STRIDER

I've heard stories - old apes tell them 'round the fire late at night - of
strange lands where the creatures can tell the future. Is that where you're
from?

WILL

In a way.. yeah, it's something like that.

Return of the Creatures

STRIDER

So what happens to it afl, to the world we've built? Tell me that.

WILL

It passes away.

Strider stares at him through the firelight.

STRIDER

History remembers, though - it's passed on, what we did, I mean?

WILL

No, Strider - there's nothing, not a trace left behind.

Strider thinks for a moment, then he smiles gently.

STRIDER

So it's just vanity then - what we believe, that the works of the ape will
last forever?

WILL

Yes, it's vanity. But not just of apes, Strider -maybe of men, too.

Return of the Creatures

He turns and settles down on his makeshift bed. Strider - the food forgotten - stares out into the night. A million stars hang on a velvet sky.

Look down from them - in the vast blackness of the forest, one tiny lightthe flickering fire.

DUST SWIRLING, HOOVES POUNDING

battalions of ape cavalry sweep out of the stables. Dawn is breaking across the city. Ma-Gog stands on a ridge, his staff raised, blessing the army as it rides out.

At its head is Drak. He clatters across the iron and wood bridge and down the avenue of idols. Votive fires burn in front of every statue.

A RAINBOW

arches across the end of a tiny gorge. Dozens of streams cascade into pools, spilling over ledges and swirling into ponds. Aragorn leads Will and Strider along a hidden, path - a rock ledge that runs behind the waterfalls.

The ledge widens into a large cave. Sunlight streams through a veil of cascading water. Aragorn looks around - something's worrying him.

ARAGORN

This is the Rainbow Tribe's cave. They should be here.

A STONE FIREPLACE

Aragorn places his hand on the circle of stones, feeling its warmth.

ARAGORN (CONT'D)

They left at the rising of the sun.

He moves deeper into the cave - a maze of limestone caverns and passage-ways. He stops at sleeping area - weapons lie there, food in baskets.

ARAGORN

(softly)

Why such hurry?

Suddenly he stops, listening. He looks at Strider -

Return of the Creatures

ARAGORN (CONT'D)

You heard it?

Strider nods his head - yes. Will hasn't heard a thing. He listens hard -
nothing.

ARAGORN (CONT'D)

Animal?

STRIDER

I don't think so.

Strider moves silently to the side of the cave. He picks up a crossbow.

STRIDER (CONT'D)

Is there another entrance?

ARAGORN

From the ridge above. Apes?

STRIDER

Scouts probably.

He cocks the crossbow. Aragorn has picks up a bow and spear. He moves towards a cavern, signaling Strider to take a passageway.

Will grabs a crossbow. Strider
tosses him a chain mail vest -
armor. They
move off.

HONEYCOMB OF PASSAGES

eep in the cave. A sound - pebbles
falling off a ledge. Then we see a
flicker of light - a torch is
moving through a cavern. Whoever
holds it,
turns a corner and is lost in
darkness.

A CROSSROADS

of arches and stalactites. Will and
Strider split apart. Will moves
silently through the darkness, into
a cavern. Through an archway he
sees a
shadow on the wall! He goes fast
towards it -

A HUGE BOULDER

The shadow comes round the boulder.
We tilt down and now we see who's
holding the torchDiamondl She's
armed with a crossbow - cocked end
loaded.
She turns a corner -

Ten feet in front of her is Strider. She stares at the massive ape's back -
a bandoleer of arrows slung over his shoulder. Her eyes widen with fear.
She raises the crossbow -

Strider hears it. He spins, weapon rising -

turns into a passage midway between them. He sees Diamond about to fire. He
screams -

Too late - she pulls the trigger! Will hurls himself forward - in front of
Strider. Whack! The arrow blasts into his chest. He crashes to the ground.

Diamond stares down at him.

DIAMOND

Will!

His eyes open - he's gasping for breath from the impact. He and Diamond
look at one another. Strider reaches down and rips the arrow out of Will's
chain mail armor. Diamond's shoulders sag with relief.

DIAMOND (CONT'D)

(indicates Strider Who's he?

WILL

I'll explain later.

He struggles to his feet and looks at Diamond -

WILL (CONT'D)

What made you come? I thought the mDNA was just a theory. One of dozens of
theories - isn't that what you said?

DIAMOND

We did a lot of work. I guess I was wrong.

WILL

People have been wrong about a lot of things.

THE GREAT VALLEY

stretches out below - primordial forests and cascading streams. Will and
Diamond stand on a rock ledge outside the cave.

Return of the Creatures

WILL (CONT'D)

This is the rift valley in Kenya -

He points at the towering, snow-capped peak.

WILL (CONT'D)

That's Kilamanjaro - ten thousand feet higher but a hundred thousand years
of wind and rain will turn it into the mountain we know. Think of it - we've come back a hundred thousand years! Everyone told me it couldn't be
done, but we've crossed the frontier now - Man has traveled through space
and time. How long has science dreamed of that?

DIAMOND

How long have you?

WILL

All my life.

DIAMOND

Dream no more. You've done it. Like you said in your note - it was Doctor

Return of the Creatures

Robert Plant of UC Berkeley.

WILL turns and looks out at the valley -

WILL

(softly)

Yeah - I really have, haven't I?

Diamond watches him. There's a shout from inside the cave -

STRIDER (O.S.)

Aragorn - I've found it!

A CAVE PAINTING

Newly-drawn, is hidden in e nook high up in the main cave. Strider, Will
and Diamond watch aa Aregorn looks at it by torchlight.

ARAGORN

I thought they would leave word for their hunters. Kip-Kena has called a
gathering of the Seven Tribes.

WILL

Where?

ARAGORN

Two days' travel - at the Eagle's Nest.

He looks out through the mouth of the cave - twilight is closing in.

ARAGORN (CONT'D)

We'll stay hera tonight. Be ready to leave at first light.

THE EMBERS OF A FIRE

burn in the circle of stones. Aragorn and Strider are sleeping next to it.
Will and Diamond have been awake all night. They sit in the shadows near
the entrance to the cave, speaking quietly.

DIAMOND

An ape civilization? You said there was a city.., what happened to it all?

WILL

You know what we've found of Aragorn's whole race? Seventeen bones, that's

all. Anthropologists have
discovered evidence of the apes -
we call them
skulls. Bones last a lot longer
than civilizations.

DIAMOND

I guess there's a lesson in that.

WILL

Listen, Billie - the apes have
discovered a disease.

Diamond reacts. Will crouches down
- in the dirt he scratches out a
small
chain of circles. It's a molecule.

WILL (CONT'D)

It's really rare and, lucky for
them, it's in an isolated area.
They're not
stupid - they understand it's
potential. They plan to give it to
the tribes
-

He draws an arrow from the molecule
to a bow-legged stick figure of a
man.

WILL (CONT'D)

Return of the Creatures

And maybe they do, but it doesn't matter -Aragorn's people aren't us. Already evolution's taken another track -

scratches a cross through the bow-legged man. He draws the figure of an
upright human.

WILL (CONT'D)

Somewhere in the rift valley is someone like us - the first man.

DIAMOND

Woman. You said it was in the mitochondrial DNA - it has to be a woman.

She reaches forward and scratches long hair on to the figure's head.

WILL

You're right. Sooner or later the apes find her. She doesn't look like the
tribes but the apes don't care - she's human.

So they give her the disease. She's different though - it doesn't work, or

at least it doesn't seem to. It gets integrated into her. It's passed on,
it mutates, it weaves its way into the mDNA. It lies there - a bomb waiting
to go off. And then one day -

DIAMOND

After a hundred thousand years?

WILL

The planet's five billion years old. What's that to Nature? A blink of the
eye.

Will throws the stick down on the ground.

WILL (CONT'D)

That's the theory, anyway.

DIAMOND

(impressed)

A helluva theory, Doctor Plant.

HE TURNS AND LOOKS IT HER -

DIAMOND (CONT'D)

Return of the Creatures

There's not much time, Will. We have to find her before the apes and we
have to do it within four weeks.

WILL

Jesus, Billie! Four weeks? We've got a theory - that's all. We don't even
know half the problems we're dealing with. You can't put a deadline on
science.

DIAMOND

Science, Will? What about people? Isn't that what this is all about. I'm
sorry - I thought there were children dying.

WILL

Sure. Of course it's about that too.

DIAMOND

But then, you don't care muchabout people do you?

THEY LOOK AT ONE ANOTHER. A BEAT. WILL'S VOICE IS HARD -

WILL

Return of the Creatures

No - I guess I don't. Not for a
long time. Ideas and knowledge are what
matter. They're the shining ideals.
That's the only way we progress.

DIAMOND

Progress to what? We're both
children of our age, aren't we?
We've grown up
to believe the more we know, the
more advanced we are. But what does that
mean if we've forgotten the things
of real value. You know the reason I
came? It's got nothing to do with
science or knowledge. I'm going to have a
child -that's why I'm here.

They look at one another.

DIAMOND (CONT'D)

Uke you said, the women's out there
somewhere. Why ere we traveling with
them?

(indicates Aragore and Strider)

We should cut ourselves loose.

WILL

We wouldn't last a day. We've got to keep moving, Billie. The apes are like
storm-troopers.

DIAMOND

Where are they now?

WILL

Right behind. I think Strider has some sort of tribal intuition. He says he
can hear their hoof beats in his head.

The first rays of dawn pierce the mist from the waterfall. Will and Diamond
turn at a sound behind them - Aragorn is getting up.

ARAGORN

Ready?

A SPARKLING RIVER

winds through a beautiful valley. The two horses splash along the water's
edge. Strider and Aragorn are mounted on one, Will and Diamond on the

other. They turn a curve - Aragorn leads them out of the shallows and into
the forest.

THE CAVE OF THE RAINBOW

Ape soldiers are swarming over the cave. A TRACKER uses torchlight to study
footprints. He looks up at Orak -

TRACKER

There's four of them, my Lord.

DRAK

Four? The Tracker points It a at of prints -

TRACKER

It's woman. Blue Eyes has a mate.

DRAK

Excellent. I look forward to meeting her.

SOLDIER (O.S.)

My Lord - hoof prints.

Drak turns - the man stands on a path that curves up towards the roof of

the cave. Drak looks up - high above he sees a slash of daylight. It's
another entrance.

DRAK

Malakai! Bolag!

Two heavily-armed officers emerge from among the soldiers. With Drak they
run for the wall. They leap up the rock face - their massive hands grabbing
tiny ledges.

Other apes follow them. They scramble up the wall with amazing speed.

AN EAGLE CIRCLES

Soaring and hovering in the sky. We tilt down a tribesman - dressed in skins edged with feathers - is perched high on a jagged peak. He's a
LOOKOUT. He tenses -

Four figures on foot appear on a path cut into the side of a cliff. The
Lookout gives a piercing crythe sound of an eagle. It carries down to -

Return of the Creatures

SERIES OF WOODEN PLATFORMS

are built into the rocky crags,
opening into caves. They are connected by
ladders and bridges slung across
dizzying drops. The inhabitants here live
with their totem -this is the nest
of the Tribe of the Eagle.

The platforms and caves are crowded
with the gathering tribes. People turn
at the Lookout's cry. A man pushes
through, listening - it's Kip-Kena.

THE LOOKOUT POST

Kip follows the direction of the
Lookout's pointing finger. Will and
Diamond lead the other two - all on
foot now - along the path.

KIP

It's the traveler! With a woman...

The Lookout shields his eyes
against the sun - the visitors ere coming
closer.

LOOKOUT

The fool - he's brought an ape with
him! He reaches for a bow but Kip's

hand falls on his arm, stopping him.

KIP

Who's the other one, though?

(realizing)

Aragorn!

He turns, yelling down to the platforms -

KIP (CONT'D)

It's the Ranger! The Ranger is free!

ON THE PLATFORMS

The tribes-people burst into action - running for the bridges, scaling the
ladders.

A WOODEN BRIDGE SWINGS THROUGH THE AIR

Whack! It locks into place on the far side of a deep crevasse. It's a primitive drawbridge. Aragorn steps on to it, leading the others across.

Return of the Creatures

The tribes-people are gathering, eager to greet him. Then they see Strider.
A ripple of fear and anger runs through them.

ARAGORN

The ape travels with me - treat him as a friend.

Nobody argues with the Ranger. He stops in front of Kip. The young warrior
starts to bow his head but Aragorn stops him. He puts out his arms - they
embrace.

Will crosses the bridge. Kip sees him. He grasps Will's arm in greeting -

KIP

You carry part of my spirit with you -I owe you my life. Welcome, Traveler.

INSIDE THE EAGLE'S NEST

A series of caves, connected by vaulted arches, extend in to the mountain.
They're crowded with members of various tribes - children are playing,

flint-knappers are fashioning
tools, women ara cooking.

A shaft of sunlight strikes a ledge
high up the wall. Kip and Will have
found a quiet place amid the
bustle.

WILL

Are the seven tribes here?

KIP

All except the Antelope. They hunt
the plains far to the west - they have
the longest journey.

WILL

Will they come?

KIP

Who knows - maybe the apes have
found them. Nobody has seen them
for many
summers gone. Why?

WILL

I'm searching for someone - a young
woman. She looks like us ...

(he indicates Diamond))

Return of the Creatures

I thought she might live with the tribes.

KIP

Is she a relative - was she born to your hearth?

WILL

To all of our hearths. My race reveres her. We think of her as the first
woman. Without her. our lives are nothing.

KIP

(nodding his head)

Women are of the spirit - we believe that. too. Mother Earth mates with the
totems. Only through woman can their children walk the world.

WILL

Have you seen her?

KIP

NO.

WILL

Return of the Creatures

You're sure? Perhaps some of the women have seen something?

KIP

She looks like you, you say? No offense, Traveler, but the women say you're
the ugliest man they've ever seen. A woman that looks like you - I'm sure
they would have talked about it.

WILL

Ugly?

They smile at one another.

KIP

I'm sorry I can't help.

A torch flares below. Kip looks down into an adjoining cave. It's empty
except for a group of men - all warriors - filing in. These are the leaders
of each of the tribes.

ANOTHER TORCH IS LIT

They ring the walls of the small cave. By their light we see the skins, the

feathers and the symbols of each
tribe's totem - the eagle, the
tiger, the
rainbow...

Beneath each one squats its leader.
One place is empty - the Tribe of
the
Antelope. Will sits near the
entrance. He watches Aragorn -
dressed in
ceremonial robes, the Crescent of
Light glistening at his neck - rise
to
his feet.

ARAGORN

We've traveled without rest - there
are soldiers a day behind. The ape
says
it's an army.

KIP

And there are more coming from the
north. Five squadrons et least, the
runners say. It's led by the old
warrior Nazgul.

ARAGORN

Is that why you called the
gathering?

KIP

Return of the Creatures

Great things are moving, Ranger -

An old man, battle-scarred and gray, leans forward. He is the leader of the
Rainbow.

A RAINBOW

A stranger walks out of the west, the moon hides the sun, armies are on the
march - come the new moon, nothing in Middle Earth will be the same.

Others nod their heads in agreement.

KIP (CONT'D)

We either fight or flee - the Tribes must decide.

ARAGORN

I know you, Kip - you always were a fighter. What do the others say?

warrior in a feathered cloak speaks -

EAGLE

It doesn't matter what we say - the Ranger has returned. We'll follow wherever he leads.

Return of the Creatures

Aragorn looks at their faces.
Slowly he shakes his head -

ARAGORN

I'll walk the path Mother Earth has
laid for me, but I'll walk it no
more
as Ranger.

The leaders stare at him. Several
start to object but he silences
them with
his hand -

ARAGORN

A man leads from his heart and
winter has come early to mine.

(softly)

I took the life of my daughter -
and some of your kinfolk with it. I
did my
duty -nothing more can be asked of
I men. But now others must walk in
my
place.

He walks forward, unfastening the
Crescent of Light. He stops in
front of
Kip -

ARAGORN

Return of the Creatures

If I should have had a son, I would have hoped for a man as fine as you.
This is my last act as Ranger of the Easterlings-

He reaches out and slips the Crescent of Light around Kip's neck.

ARAGORN (CONT'D)

Take care of my father's people. Guide them well.

(he looks at the leaders)

You must decide what is best for the Tribes. For me... I was the one that
had to strike the blow, but it was the apes who killed my child. Tomorrow I
will go to fight them. What father could do any less?

He turns away and walks towards the entrance. Only Will sees the tears in
his eyes.

KIDS' FACES, WIDE-EYED

They huddle together - staring at the strange-looking woman and the ape.

Return of the Creatures

Strider is building a small fire at the side of the cave, Diamond lays down
furs for sleeping. , She looks up - the leaders are coming out of the meeting. Will approaches.

WILL

They're going to war. They leave at dawn.

STRIDER

They'll be slaughtered.

WILL

They think if they leave the valley, their totems won't follow. Without
them, they say they're dead anyway.

DIAMOND

We should go now.

Will looks at her. She meets his gaze. Suddenly she realizes -

DIAMOND

Oh, no! We're not fighting someone else's war -

WILL

Return of the Creatures

Listen to me -

DIAMOND

We've got four weeks, Willl Four
weeks to find her. She's not here,
so whet
are we waiting for? Let's go!

The tribes-people turn at the
raised voices. Will takes Diamond's
arm and
guides her to a private corner -

WILL

Listen, Billie! We know the future
- but if we beat the apes, they
can't
harm the woman.

DIAMOND

Beat the apes?! And say we don't -
or say one of us gets captured.
What
then? Don't you understand? Four
weeksi

WILL

Yeah, I understand - but those
things aren't going to happen. We
know
things the apes can't even dream
of. This is our world, Billie - men
won it

with their minds. All we need is knowledge and science. We've got them
both. We can win!

DIAMOND

What are we going to do - dazzle them with calculus? This is an army, Will
- you said it yourself. Storm-trooperst

WILL

Look -

He bends and picks up s rock from the ground. He hands it to Diamond -

WILL (CONT'D)

Taste it. That's saltpeter - the natural form of potassium nitrate. The
caves are littered with the stuff. You've smelt the air - there's sulfur
all around. If we burn timber, that'Il give us charcoal. You're s scientist
- you know what it means.

Sure - she knows what it means. She stares at him.

Return of the Creatures

DIAMOND

It's strange, isn't it? Give s man s problem and the first thing he thinks
about is weapons.

WILL

We're a frail species, Billea. It's only weapons that have made us bigger
than we are.

DIAMOND

Or smaller.

WILL

It's the apes who are going to be a whole lot smaller after this. We can
beat themi No more experiments - no more problem.

DIAMOND

(quietly)

I hope your right, Will.

FIRES BURN

all over the eagle's nest, turning piles of timber into charcoal. The camp

Return of the Creatures

is a hive of activitycolumns of
tribes-people make their way up
from the
valley carrying piles of sulfur
rock; women and children sit in
circles,
pounding the saltpeter into dust.
Will moves among the tribal
leaders,
watching as they measure and
combine the elements in bowls.

Strider sits apart, watching, not
sure if the humans have lost their
minds.

STRAW MAN FLIES TOWARDS US

He looks like a scarecrow except
he's dressed in captured ape armor.
Rigged
to a flying fox, he speeds past a
rock face. All of the tribes-people
are
gathered on the side of a crevasse,
watching.

The straw men flies closer -
towards a rocky outcrop. Will
touches a
burning ember to the ground. We see
a flash of flame as a fuse ignites
but
we lose it among the rocks. A thin
trail of smoke marks its passage.

Return of the Creatures

The tribes-people watch - nothing seems to be happening. Suddenly - just as
the straw man reaches the outcrop -

Ka-boom! A huge explosion. Fire and flying rock hit the straw men.

The tribes-people scream.
Terrified, they turn and run. Smoke and dust
obscure the flying fox. Will walks forward to examine his handiwork.

Tribes-people peer out from their hiding places - the smoke and dust clear.
They see the tattered shreds of the straw man hanging from the rope.
Several of the women start to cry in fear.

Will stands on the edge of the crevasse. He turns - Kip, Aragorn and the
other leaders are approaching. They look at him with trepidation.

KIP

You make fire from rocks of the earth -what is this thing?

WILL

Gunpowder.

Return of the Creatures

Kip turns to the others. They repeat the word, as if that will unlock its
mystery.

WILL (CONT'D)

We've still got work to do.

He turns and goes. The tribespeople, emboldened by their leaders, come
closer. They draw back from Will as he makes his way through them. He comes
face to face with Strider. The man and the ape look at one another.

STRIDER

Apes believe men are the devil's children. Maybe they're right. What have
you done, Will - what have you unleashed on the world?

WILL

Nothing, Strider. The future, that's all.

STRIDER

I can't fight with you tomorrow, Will. To kill an ape in a brawl is one

Return of the Creatures

thing, but I can't go to war
against my people.

WILL

(kindly)

I never expected you to.

Again they look at one another.
Will turns and leaves.

WATER FLYING, HOOVES POUNDING

Drak and his cavalry, pennants
flying, gallop along the edge of a
river.
Ranks of infantry, followed by
horse-drawn supply wagons, travel
behind.

The river swings around a point
thick with trees. We crane up above
the
foliage - a tributary flows clown
the other side. Marching through
the
shallows is another army of apes.
At their head, on a stallion, is
Nazgul.

The two squadrons converge at the
end of the point. The foot soldiers
meld
together, the Praetorian Guard
splash ahead, Drak and Nazgul ride
side by

Return of the Creatures

side. Ahead, the river and its tributary pour over a broad rock ledge. It's
a natural weir -

THE FORD OF THE THREE RIVERS

A jumble of logs and broken branches lie snagged in the middle of the
river. The Praetorian Guard sweep past them and turn on to the weir.

The Guard spur their horses forward, forcing them through the fast-running
current, crossing to the other side -

IN THE TREES

A shadow of movement. Tribesmen glide through the dappled light of the
forest, almost invisible in skins and camouflage.

Will and Kip stand motionless, deep in shadow. They watch as the Guard on
their horses come thundering across the ford, straight towards them. The
infantry are close behind. Will drops his hand -

TRAILS OF FIRE

whip along the ground - out of the forest and on to the flattened rocks
that form part of the ford. The Guards' horses shy away. The apes look down
in puzzlement -

Boom! Boom! Booml Sections of the weir explode in plumes of rock and water.
Apes are cut to pieces, horses are hurled into the fast-flowing water.

On the far side - Orak's horse rears up. He drives his spurs into its
flanks, trying to control it. Clouds of dust and smoke billow across the
weir, the wounded are screaming - the ape cavalry wheel and turn in confusion.

Drak plunges forward - chaos all around him. He pounds his chest with both
fists and roars -

DRAK

Apes - chargel

The apes still on their horses hear his cry. They spur their mounts forward. The first of the cavalry reach -

THE SHORE

Boom... boom! More explosions rip the river bank to pieces.

IN THE FOREST

Batteries of cross-bows are mounted on a series of long wooden frames. The
Eagle leader and his warriors run from one to the other, touching flames to
rope fuses. Fire sizzles towards the crossbows, each one loaded with a
charge -

Bam...bam...bamf The scores of crossbows fire.

ON THE FORD

The ape cavalry are plunging through the smoke and debris. Wham! The hail
of arrows cut them to pieces.

Drak is in the middle of a whirling mass of apes and horses. He looks
through the smoke - into the forest. He sees Will, standing on a rock with

Return of the Creatures

Kip, like a general commanding his army.

Drak bellows with rage. He snaps the reins, about to drive his horse onward. An arrow flies in from the flank. Whackt It slams into Drak's chest
armor, splintering. He turns -

THE JUMBLE OF LOGS

floats in the middle of the river. The leader of the Rainbow Tribe, water
streaming off of him, kneels on the tangle of trees and branches, reloading
his bow. This is no jumble of logs - it's a firing platform they've anchored therel

dozen Rainbow warriors, hidden in the water, clamber out of the river. They
kneel next to their leader, drlwing their bows -

THE FORD

Drak watches es I flight of arrows slam into the milling ranks of apes.
Right in front of him, an arrow rips through the throat of the leader of

the Praetorian Guard. Drak turns to Nazgul, yelling -

DRAK

The ones in the river - take themi Nazgul spurs his horse back across the
weir.

ON THE SHORE

Ape cavalry and infantry scramble up the river bank. Bam! They hear the
charges go off - the hurl themselves down. Another volley of arrows scythes
through them -

IN THE FOREST

The Eagle leader and his men work feverishly to reload and recharge the
batteries of crossbows. One of the warriors looks up - terror on his face.

Drak, followed by the remnants of his Praetorian Guard, charge through the
blue haze of gunsmoke - straight towards them.

Return of the Creatures

One of the crossbow batteries fires! Arrows hit his horse's armor but Drak
doesn't falter. Crouched Iow in the saddle, he spins the Gatling gun like a
gunslinger. He locks it under his arm.

The eagle warriors start to break and run. The apes' horses sound like
thunder rolling closer. The Eagle leader and several of his warriors stand
their ground, desperately working to reload.

They spin the battery, sighting straight at Drak's chest. They fire! Arrows
fly -

Drak leaps out of the saddle! He catches hold of an overhanging bough. The
arrows whiz underneath, skimming his butt. He leaps again - higher into the
tree.

The Eagle leader looks up - sunlight sparkles on the leaves. It's dazzling
-

Return of the Creatures

Smash! Drak's sword cleaves through one of the warriors. Drak has dropped
to the ground, right behind them. The Eagle leader turns - too late!
Rat-a-tat-tat! The Gatling gun fires. Arrows shred the Eagle leader's
feathered coat. He crumples to the ground like some fallen bird.

THE FORD

The ape infantry pour across the ford, charging over the bodies of their
fallen comrades.

THE FOREST

Riderless horses, part of the ape cavalry, charge wildly through the trees.
We tilt up - their riders have abandoned them and taken to the trees. The
branches are thick with apes firing, cutting down groups of running
tribesmen.

THE ROCK PLATFORM

Will and several tribesmen hurl camouflage aside revealing a long iron

barrel wedged in the rocks. One of
the warriors tilts it up, aiming it at
the trees; another stokes pebbles
and scraps of metal into the
barrel.

Will touches an ember to a fuse.
Everyone dives for cover -

Boom! The primitive cannon fires.
The shrapnel hits the trees. Shredded
apes, branches and leaves fall to
the ground.

Will and the warriors reload. Again
they fire - but the charge is too big.
The whole cannon breaks free of the
rocks. It flies like a missile and
smashes into the trunk of a tree.
Timber!

A ROCKY GORGE

Its rugged walls are lined with
piles of huge boulders. Aragorn and
a group
of warriors are fighting hand-to-
hand, being forced back by scores
of ape
infantry.

Aragorn drives his spear at a huge
ape. The point plunges into the
animal's

belly, up and under his armor.
Blood spurts out from the joins in the
metal.

IN THE TREES

An ape sharpshooter sights down his
crossbow - straight at Aragorn. He fires -

AMONG THE BOULDERS

Wham! The crossbow bolt smashes
into Aragorn's shoulder, sending him
reeling. One of the tribesmen turns
- it's Kip. He sees Aragorn on his
knees.

Kip wields a sword, fighting his
way towards Aragorn. Slash! He takes one
ape across the chest. Whaml Another
ape in the neck. He grabs Aragorn and
starts to drag him out of the melee.

IN THE TREES

The ape sharpshooter has Kip in his
sights. His finger reaches for the
trigger. He starts to squeeze -

Sswhishl The sound of an arrow.
Whackl It buries itself in the

sharpshooter's neck. He falls out of the tree -

HIGH AMONG THE BOULDERS

Will. He stands almost at the top of the gorge, lowering a crossbow. He
looks down at Kip's men - the apes, vastly superior in numbers, are swarming forward, driving the tribesmen back.

On a ridge below him, four tribesmen scramble away from huge boulder. A
flash of fire then - Ka-bam!

ON THEGROUND

Apes are rushing forward. They hear the explosion. Several apes turn - the
huge boulder, split into chunks, flies towards them. The apes scatter.
Smashl The chunks knock apes aside like skittles.

But there's more of them behind, spilling in to the gorge, over-running it
-

THE DUST FROM THE EXPLOSION

Return of the Creatures

swirls past Drak. He looks up - he sees Will on the ridge, silhouetted against the sky.

Drak snarls deep in his throat. He wheels his horse and gallops hard towards a trail that winds up among the boulders.

ON THE RIDGE

Will moves fast along the top of the ridge. He stops - looking down on the
river. On the other side, Nazgul and a platoon of apes unload huge leather
bladders from the wagons and empty them into the river.

Will shades hil ayes - the water glistens with iridescent colors. He realizes - it's oil.

The current carries it straight towards the platform in the river. The
warriors of the Rainbow tribe - unaware - are still aboard, firing at the
apes on the ford.

Will turns fait - wa whip pan along the shoreline. He sees what he feared -

Return of the Creatures

two apes below him with a fire burning. They slot flaming arrows into their
crossbows -

Will unslings his crossbow, steadies himself and fires -

Ks-whack! The arrow rips through one ape's neck. He pitches forward -
heed-first into the fire. The other ape hurls himself aside, diving for cover.

Will re-loads. The side of the ape's head is just visible behind a rock. If
Will makes this, it's going to be a helluva shot.

His finger curls around the trigger - right behind him, the sound of hooves. Will spins

it's Drak charging towards him. He raises the Gatling gun -

Will aims at the big ape's throat and fires.

Drak swerves. The arrow misses his throat but slams into his exposed forearm. The Gatling gun flies from his hand.

Return of the Creatures

There's no time for Will to re-load
- he turns and runs.

Drak charges down on him. He draws
a harpoon out of its scabbard.

Will scrambles over a crest -
nothing but thin air!

Drak has him square in his sights.
He draws back his arm, about to
hurl the
harpoon. Will throws himself
forward -

THE SIDE OF A CLIFF

Will falls down, down, down.

Drak reins his horse to a halt
right at the edge. He looks over -
Will
plunges towards the river, flowing
fast below the ford.

Splash! Will cannonballs into the
water and disappears. Drak stares
down,
trying to catch sight of him.
Nothing.

IN THE RIVER

A tree branch and other flotsam is
being carried downstream by the
current.

Return of the Creatures

A pair of hands emerge from the water and grab hold of it. Will's head
follows.

Gasping, catching his breath, he looks upstream - the water pours over the
weir. A flaming arrow arcs through the air. The ape on the shore has done
his job -

THE OIL SLICK

erupts in flames as the arrow hits it. The whole surface of the river is
suddenly transformed into a raging blaze.

The Rainbow leader and his men turn. They see a wall of flame racing
towards them. Several warriors dive into the water, swimming for the shore
-

Whoosh! The flames engulf them. A wall of fire sweeps over the wooden platform. Like macabre shadows - we see the dancing shapes of the dying warriors.

IN THE RIVER

Return of the Creatures

The current pulls Will down the river. He looks back - the molten fire
spills over the weir. Anguished screams are carried on the wind. A pillar
of black, oily smoke rises up high into the sky -

THE EAGLES' NEST

The platforms and rocky outcrops are crowded with the women, children and
old folks. Diamond and Strider stand together. All of them stare down at
the river valley. The pillar of smoke rises higher.

WOMAN (O.S.)

They're here!

Diamond turns - the woman is standing on the highest platform. Diamond
follows the direction of her outstretched arm.

A group of warriors, followed by their women-folk and children, are coming
round the mountain path. Their leader wears a golden fur and a head-dress

of auroch's horns. It's the Tribe of the Antelope.

OUTSIDE THE MAIN CAVE

A chorus of chattering voices. The new arrivals are surrounded by members
of their sister tribes. The leader of the Antelope stands in the center,
listening to a woman -Kip's wife. Whatever she's saying is lost in the
hubbub.

ANTELOPE

Quiet!

Instantly, the voices die.

ANTELOPE (CONT'D)

(anxious)

Where?

Kip's wife doesn't answer - she walks forward and points to the pillar of
smoke. The Antelope leader turns to his warriors.

ANTELOPE (CONT'D)

We go - now!

Return of the Creatures

DIAMOND AND STRIDER

stand on the platform, watching several old men lower the drawbridge.
Whack! It locks into place. The antelope warriors cross it and disappear
down a narrow trail.

The rest of the Antelope tribe move towards the cave. Diamond turns away -
then she stops. Something has caught her eye. She stares at the crowd of
women and children heading into the cave.

STRIDER

What is it?

Diamond doesn't answer - she tenses. In the milling crowd of brown bodies,
she sees it again - a flash of gold. It*s sunlight on blonde hair.

DIAMOND

She's here.., holy God - she's herel It's not a woman - it's a child!

Return of the Creatures

She grabs a rope ladder, ignores the rungs and slithers down it.

A YOUNG GIRL

helps her mother set up camp. She is about 10 years old, tawny-haired,
taller and straighter-backed'than any of her people. She looks like us.

Diamond pushes through the women and kids gathered around the hearth. She
stops. The young girl turns. For a moment she and Diamond stare at one another, separated by a hundred thousand years, but so similar they can
both see themselves in the other.

THE YOUNG GIRL SMILES. DIAMOND RETURNS IT -

DIAMOND

What's your name?

The girl's mother stares, amazed to see someone who looks like her child.

MOTHER

Her name is Aiv.

Return of the Creatures

DIAMOND

Ev?

(Realizing)

Of course. My people have a name like that - "Eve" is how we say it.

The mother nods - the sound seems to please her. Diamond puts out her arms
and indicates the young girl. The mother smiles, giving her permission.
Diamond puts her arms around Eve.

DIAMOND (CONT'D)

(softly)

I've come a long way to find you.

Eve looks at her - wide-eyed, innocent.

EVE

Why?

DIAMOND

To keep you safe.

She holds her tight. The mother catches Diamond's eye.

Return of the Creatures

MOTHER

Do you have children?

Diamond shakes her head - no. The mother can't hide her disappointment.

DIAMOND

What's wrong?

MOTHER

I was hoping you had a son. Aiv's a sweet girl. She's the child of my heart. But the way she looks, nobody will want her as a mate.

Before Diamond can answer there's a commotion outside the cave. She turns
to look - Strider and tribes-people are running out into the daylight.

SWIRLS OF DUST

rise up from I mountain path. Whatever's causing it is hidden from view by
the peaks and crags. The tribal-people gather on vantage points, watching
it come closer. Strider cocks his head - listening. A shadow of fear passes
across his face.

Return of the Creatures

STRIDER

Horses! It's horses!

Horses mean apesi Panic sweeps
through the tribes-people. Women grab their
children, young kids start screaming, old men and boys scramble for
weapons.

Diamond weaves through the flying mass of people. She swings up on to a
platform beside Strider. He points -

Coming into view on the mountain path - running and stumbling, dragging
their wounded - are what's left of the Antelope warriors.

Their women-folk cry out as they realize what has happened to their mates.
The warriors race along the path and across the drawbridge. Nobody raised
it when they left -

Several old men and a couple of boys struggle now to do it. They haul on the ropes and pulleys. It starts to swing upwards -

Here he comes - Drak! He's galloping hard at the head of his cavalry,
battle scarred and bloodied. He sees the drawbridge starting to lift. He
doesn't pause - he whips his horse into a thundering gallop.

The bridge rises higher. Drak's horse leaps! It soars across the crevasse -
the giddylng drop stretches out below - and lands on the lifting bridge.

The men and boys stare in horror. Orak charges down on them. They back away
-all except one boy, not even in his teens, who stands his ground.

Swish! Drak's sword cleaves him from shoulder to waist. The other tribesmen
run. Wham! The drawbridge falls back into place. The ape cavalry charge
across it.

BROAD WOODEN PLATFORM

Return of the Creatures

An ape horseman flies across the platform. He leaps off the edge, on to a
lower platform. Diamond's right in front of him!

She throws herself aside, grabs hold of a rope ladder and drops onto -

A ROCK SHELF

She looks across the broad area in front of the cave - apes everywhere,
weapons flashing, people screaming.

A young boy tries to out-run an ape warrior - it's Gray Beard. The young
boy hasn't got a chance. Gray Beard lashes out at him with a stock-whip.

It curls around the boy's ankle, tripping him. The boy looks up - he tries
to shield his face. Too late! The horse's hooves smash down -

Diamond looks away, unable to watch. She sees Eve. The young girl is at the
front of the cave, spinning in panic. Her mother runs towards her...

Return of the Creatures

The mother doesn't see Gray Beard galloping towards her. Diamond screams a
warning but it's just one more cry in the commotion.

Gray Beard raises a short-handled lance and hurls it like a javelin. It
hits the mother in the small of the back, straight through the spine. She
pitches forward - dead. Eve screams and runs towards her mother.

Diamond leaps off the rock ledge -

IN FRONT OF THE CAVE

Diamond runs faster than she's ever run, sprinting to grab Eva. Drak wheels
his horse - he sees Diamond. His lip curls back and he smiles - one of the
Blue Eyes! And a woman! He leaps his horse forward -

DRAK

Grab the female!

Gray Beard is off his horse. Diamond runs towards him. He raises a
crossbow...

Return of the Creatures

Drak charges down on her from behind. He holds the harpoon at his shoulder.
He aims at her legs.

Diamond races on - her only thought, to save Eve. It'll never happen -
she's as good as deadGray Beard's in front, aiming. Drak's right behind. He
hurls the harpoon.

Whoosh! Strider swings through the air. He clings to one of the rope ladders - it's like Tarzan, except he's an ape. He grabs Diamond by the
scruff of the neck and yanks her out of the way.

Drak's harpoon skims past them. Gray Beard stares in amazement at the woman
flying through the air. But that's not his big surprise - with Diamond out
of the way, the harpoon is flying straight at him. He screams as it rips
into his throat.

HIGH ROCK LEDGE

Strider - Diamond clutched under his arm - lands on a ledge high above the

Return of the Creatures

fight. Diamond turns fast and looks back -

IN FRONT OF THE CAVE

Eve crouches over the body of her mother. The woman's mouth is frozen in an
anguished scream, her dead eyes stare straight ahead. Eva shakes her,
desperately hoping for some sign of life. Nothing. Eve starts to cry.

A dark shadow falls across her. She looks up - it's Drak. He reaches down
and grabs her by the neck. He beats his chest with his fist and raises her
up above his head like a trophy.

ON THE ROCK LEDGE

Diamond, anguished, tries to go to the little girl but Strider holds her in
an iron grip. He swings Diamond off her feet, and leaps for an overhanging
branch of a tree. He jumpsfrom the tree to a jagged peak and vanishes from
sight.

CHARRED AND SMOKING WRECKAGE

Return of the Creatures

floats at the shore of the river.
It is what remains of the firing platform
- the bodies of several of the
Rainbow warriors still on board.

Smoke curls away from the platform
and drifts through the forest. The only
sound is the whinnying of a horse -
it has a broken leg. Again and again it
tries to get to its feet.

A solitary figure makes his way
through the shadows. It's Will, soaking wet
from the river. He stops at the
entrance to the rocky gorge and looks at
the carnage all around him. So much
for knowledge and science. This is
where the warriors of the tribes
made their last stand - their bodies lie
huddled together in a jumble.

Will stares at them, anguish on his face.

WILL

(softly, to himself)

I was so sure...

Return of the Creatures

He kneels and turns one of the bodies over. It's Kip - speared through the
chest. A shaft of sunlight hits the Crescent of Light. It glints on his lifeless throat. Gently, he closes Kip's glassy eyes.

sound behind him. Will hurls himself aside, grabbing for a weapon. He looks
up -it's the Lookout, battle-stained and weary. Their eyes meet -

LOOKOUT

(quietly)

You said we'd win.

Will just nods - he knows.

LOOKOUT (CONT'D)

You gave us hope - that was the cruelest thing.

The Lookout kneels and crosses Kip's hands across his chest. He reaches
down and removes the Crescent of Light. He turns to Will -

LOOKOUT (CONT'D)

Return of the Creatures

Get the weapons you need. The apes'll be coming back for their dead. Hurry!

Will arms himself with crossbows and arrows from the bodies.

CLOUDS OF SMOKE

rise into the sky - the eagle's nest is on fire. Drak and his apes make
their way along a narrow mountain trail - they've put the humans' camp to
the torch.

With them is a long line of prisonerswomen and children mostly, many of
them in tears. They carry long poles over which are slung their dead and
dying. We crane, up to -

HUGE ROCK OVERHANG

high up the mountain-side. Standing underneath it, hidden in shadow, are
Diamond and Strider. They look down on the mountain trail. Diamond sees Eve.

THE MOUNTAIN TRAIL

Return of the Creatures

The young girl stumbles along the road, tied by a length of chain to Drak's
saddle. She's bruised and bleeding, her ankles shackled, barely able to walk.

THE ROCK OVERHANG

Diamond looks at her, close to tears, but there's nothing she can do. She
watches the convoy wind along the trail.

Boomi The fire must have hit a store of gunpowder - an explosion rips
through the eagle's nest, blowing out the side of one of the peaks. Diamond
watches the dust climb into the sky. All her hopes seem to be going with
it.

IN THE RIVER

It's twilight. Will and the Lookout are wading around a knob of land that
protects one end of a tiny beach.

Will sees a fire burning on the sand, a cave opening off the beach, piles
of stones like burial mounds.

Return of the Creatures

WILL

What is this place?

LOOKOUT

It's called the Crossroads of the
Fallen King - it's where our
forefathers
are laid to rest. It's sacred to us
- anyone who's still alive will
make
their way here.

They wade closer to the beach. In
the firelight they see groups of
tribesmen -survivors of the battle.
Women and children - the lucky few
who
managed to flee the eagle's nest -
are binding the warriors' wounds.

They look up - everyone falls
silent at the sight of Will. As he
comes
closer he recognizes a woman,
sitting alone -

WILL

It's Kip's wife. She's come from

THE EAGLE'S NEST -

Return of the Creatures

He goes towards her, passing the other tribes-people. Nobody greets him.
They just watch him pass. He stops in front of Kip's wife. Her eyes are red
from crying.

WILL

rm sorry about your mate.

She says nothing - she just stares at him. Will keeps going -

WILL (CONT'D)

I've been to the eagle's nest. I was looking for the woman I was with. We
searched but...

(he pauses)

What happened - was she captured?

KIP'S WIFE

I threw myself off a platform. I don't know what happened to anyone.

Will nods. He gets to his feet and moves to the women near the fire. We
don't hear what he says, but we know what he is asking. One after another

Return of the Creatures

they shake their heads - no, they know nothing of Diamond.

SHAFT OF MOONLIGHT

shimmers on the water. Will sits on a rock that straggles into the water.
His face is grim, his heart heavy with grief. He's making something with
his hands - twisting and turning them - but in the dim light we can't see
what it is.

INSIDE THE CAVE

A shaft of moonlight falls on a semi-circle of rock slabs standing on their
end - it's like Stonehenge. The surviving tribes-people are gathered in
their shadow.

OLD MAN

It's half a day since the battle. Any that survived would be here by now -
we are all that remains of the Seven Tribes. The Ranger himself died on the
field. We must decide ourselves what to do.

Return of the Creatures

Silence for a moment. They have spent too long following a leader for
discussion to come easily. Finally, a wounded warrior speaks -

WOUNDED WARRIOR

Like you say, Kip is dead. Maybe it's a sign -the Rangers have left Middle
Earth forever. Perhaps it's telling us to do the same.

A young woman - probably in her 20s - shakes her head.

YOUNG WOMAN

Leave the valley? This is where the eagles fly. This is their home. Nobody
can live without their totem - we all know that!

LOOKOUT

Nobody can live with the apes eitherl If we stay here, we die. But if we
travel beyond the Tower of the Moon, we've got a chance. Who knows - maybe
our totems will follow us?

Return of the Creatures

There's a murmur of agreement. It grows louder, tribes-people nodding their
heads.

THE BEACH

Now we see what Will has been making - it's a boat made out of twigs and
leaves. A tiny hull and a gaff-rigged mast. He leans forward and drops it
in the water. He watches the current carry it away. Farther and farther it
bobs out into the river -

WILL

(softly)

I'm sorry, Billie. I should have listened - it wasn't our war. All you
wanted was a baby...

He can't go on. He watches the tiny boat disappear around the knob of
land.

IN THE RIVER

The current carries the boat past a jagged boulder. An ape's hand reaches

out and picks it up. He lifts it up to look more closely. We see his face -
it's Strider. He turns the toy over in his hand, looking at it quizzically.
He hands it to Diamond, wading along behind him -

STRIDER

It looks like someone made it.

DIAMOND

It's a boat - it's gaff-rigged.

(realizing)

Oh, Jesus...

She plunges forward, wading as fast as she can.

DIAMOND (CONT'D)

Will!

ON THE BEACH

Will is walking up the beach. He stops, listening. He hears it again -his
name! He turns and heads towards the river. He sees Diamond coming round

Return of the Creatures

the headland, splashing through the water.

Will stops. They look at one another - then they both move forward, arms
stretching out. They wrap their arms around each other.

WILL

(softly)

I thought I'd lost you.

DIAMOND

I thought you were dead.

They keep holding each other.

WILL

How did you find this place?

DIAMOND

Strider. His father was a tracker. We've been following a trail for hours.

Will looks over her shoulder - Strider is wading towards them.

DIAMOND (CONT'D)

He saved my life, Will.

Return of the Creatures

Will goes to greet him. The man and the ape embrace.

WILL

Thank you, my friend - thank you.

STRIDER

What did you expect? You would have done the same for me.

SHOWER OF SPARKS

as Will puts a log on the fire. From inside the cave we hear the murmur of
voices as the argument goes back and forth.

Both Diamond and Strider are wrapped in furs - their clothes are laid out
next to the fire, drying. Will speaks to Diamond -

WILL

Some times when we want something so bad, we can take a thing and twist it
in our head. You're sure about this, Billie?

DIAMOND

Return of the Creatures

I'm pregnant, Will - I'm not crazy.
She's not like them - she's a
mutation.
Evolution's always trying to
improve on itself. It's turned out
a child
that can walk taller and run
faster, one whose brain-pan holds a
mind that
can think laterally. I've seen her,
Will. I've held her in my arms -
she
was us.

Will looks at her. There's no doubt
- he believes her.

WILL

You said she was with Drak.

DIAMOND

On a chain.

WILL

It's two days' march to the city.
Was she wounded - can she make it?

DIAMOND

She can make it.

(a beat - she looks at him)

Will?

Return of the Creatures

Before he can answer, the Old Man
and several others come down the
beach -

OLD MAN

It's decided - we're leaving the
valley forever.

(turns to Strider)

Your people have won - the Seven
Tribes of Middle Earth have been
broken.
Long may their spirits haunt you

(he turns back to Will)

You and your mate can travel with u
but we've got misery enough to
carry.
Our hearth is not home to ny ape.

WILL

Then it's not home to us. The ape's
better than any man I've known.

The Old Man's lip curls in a sneer.
He shrugs and walks away.

STRIDER

Go with them. Will - everyone needs
their own kind.

Return of the Creatures

Will and Diamond newer almost simultaneously -

WILL

No!

DIAMOND

Of course we can't...

(to Will)

The city, Will.

Will and Strider turn nd look at her - incredulous.

WILL

We call it a city - it's more like a fortress, Billie. It can't be done.

DIAMOND

The three of you got out - everyone thought that was impossible too.

WILL

We were lucky. But that's the trouble with luck - it runs out. I don't want
to be back in the city when it does.

Return of the Creatures

DIAMOND

What about Eve - what do we do, just forget about her?

WILL

No. Maybe we can't stop the apes giving her the disease - but they'll have
to turn her loose. That's the only way she can infect others. So we lay a
plan and we find her. Then it's our job to stop her having children. If we
can do that, it can't be passed on through the race.

She shrugs That's the only thing I can think of.

DIAMOND

How long will that take - less than twenty-five days ?

WILL

No.

DIAMOND So what of my child?

We have to face it - you're going to lose it.

Return of the Creatures

She turns away, trying to keep her
emotions in check. Will comes to her
side -

WILL (CONT'D)

We can't take our eye off the goal.
If we solve this, you can have other
children. Not if wa throw our lives
away, though.

DIAMOND

Whose, Will - whose children?

She looks at him. He meets her
gaze. A beat.

WILL

guess that's your call.

DIAMOND

What sort of father would you make?
You told me once the only thing that
matters is knowledge. That's wrong.
Science and technology can only take
you so far - in the end it's our
humanity that maners. That's what
makes us

Return of the Creatures

great. You're a wonderful scientist, Will -but what sort of person are you?
What would you do if it was your child?

She looks straight into his eyes. Finally he answers. Softly -

WILL

I don't know how to do it - not the humanity part, that's easy compared to
getting into the city. I just don't know...

He picks up a stick and starts to scratch out a rough map on the ground.

WILL (CONT'D)

It sits on a river. There's only one bridge -heavily guarded. Even if we
could cross it, all the ridges and roads are patrolled -

STRIDER

There's one place that's not.

Both Diamond and Will turn to him. He takes the stick -

STRIDER (CONT'D)

Down here - it's called Funeral
Rock. It sits at the bottom of the
temple.
From there you can make your way
into the city. Even so, you still
have to
cross the river.

He draws an arrow across the water,
illustrating the problem. Diamond
is
about to speak but she looks at
Will - he's staring at the arrow,
an idea,
half formed, is starting to form.

WILL

Maybe there is a way...across the
river, I mean.

DIAMOND

How?

Will turns to her -

WILL

You'll love it - there's barely any
science to it at all.

DIAMOND

We're going? Is that right - we're
going!?

Return of the Creatures

Their eyes meet and hold. He smiles at her.

THREE SILHOUETTES

travel fast along a high ridge. The sun - a fiery disc - rises right behind
them. We recognize their physiques - Will in the lead, then Diamond and
Strider. As they cross the face of the sun, we dissolve to -

LIGHTS TWINKLE

on the buildings and terraces of the apes' city. Will and his two comrades
are on a bluff, looking down. The sound of music and laughter drifts towards them on the night air. Suddenly a huge tongue of flame shoots out
of a stone chimney.

STRIDER

They've started up the furnace.

(softly)

Let the games begin.

DIAMOND

Return of the Creatures

What games?

WILL

The apes kill their prisoners for sport. The furnace takes care of the
bodies.

Diamond - sickened by it - turns to look at Will. Already he's heading off,
leading them down nrrow trail.

A HIDDEN LEDGE

much closer to the city. Will and the others move fast along it, deep in
the shadows. The river thunders by below them, separating them from the
city. The only way across is the massive iron and wood bridge. Ape guards
patrol it.

Only Diamond pauses to look et it. Will and Strider urge her forward. It
disappears from view.

A STEEL ARROW

flies through the air. Tied to its shaft, trailing out behind, is a rope

made from vines. Will lowers a
crossbow. He watches the arrow fly
through
the mist and spray -

THE RIVER

races by just below and pours over
the Falls of No Return. Whack! The
arrow
buries itself in the trunk of a
massive tree standing on the bank.

ON THE OTHER SHORE

Will and Strider haul the rope taut
and tie it round a tree. It
stretches
from one side of the river to the
other. All it has to do is hold.
Will
turns to Diamond. He shouts to be
heard over the roar of the falls -

WILL

You first. We'll be right behind.

Diamond scrambles up on to a rock
platform and grabs hold of the
rope. She
looks across the riverthe moonlight
spills through the wind-blown
spray;
the roaring water rushes by; the
rope hangs like a thread. There's
fear on

her face -

WILL (CONT'D)

You ready?

DIAMOND

It sure as shit ain't Kansas, is it?

WILL

Go!

Diamond throws herself forward. Her feet leave the platform. Hand over hand
she goes - out across the river.

Will watchel for a moment then launches himself - his hands wrap around the
rope.

Strider slings his crossbow over his shoulder and jumps. The line bows
under his weight. Diamond'l feet drop closer to the water. She looks down -
the mass of black water, flecked with foam, rushes past.

Will looks ahead - Diamond is almost lost in flurries of spray. She's dripping wet, hauling herself forward -

The sound of the Falls is deafening. Right below her, a huge, swirling
"hole" opens up. It's a whirlpool. She starts to swing across it.
Joltl

THE TREE TRUNK

The arrow pulls part way out of the tree. The steel shaft shivers but it
holds. Everything seems okay. Suddenly -

Snap! One of the strands of the vine breaks -

ON THE ROPE

Everything bucks and shudders. Diamond screams. She looks down - straight
into the vortex of the whirlpool. Her blood runs cold - she freezes.

WILL SEES HER HANGING MOTIONLESS ON THE ROPE. HE SCREAMS AT HER -

WILL

Go! Billie - go!

She doesn't seem to hear. Her eyes are wide with fear - staring down, down
into the whirlpool's bottomless well.

WILL, TRYING TO GET TO HER, HURLS HIMSELF FORWARD. THE ROPE STRAINS AND
BOWS -

WILL

Move!

She doesn't react. Strider watches as Will tries to catch up. The rope is
swaying so much it's agonizingly slow.

Diamond stares at a huge log spinning down into nothingness. The whirlpool
seems to be swallowing everything, even the moonlight -

WILL (CONT'D)

Billiai What about the baby?!

The word hits her. She pulls her eyes from the swirling death. She looks at
Will.

WILL (CONT'D)

Move, Billiel Nowl

She understands. She starts to pull herself forward. Will slumps with relief -

ON THE SHORE

The arrow moves another inch out of the trunk. The rope fixed to its shaft
is strained to breaking point. But still everything holds...

THE IRON AND WOOD BRIDGE

One of the guards patrols the bridge. Out of the corner of his eye - flash
of something. He looks towards the Falls.

GUARD

(calling)

Gimla.

The other guard joins him. They peer through the night at the spray rising
from the Falls. They see it again - above the river, a flash of light on
metal.

Return of the Creatures

The keep watching. An eddy of wind clears the mist for a second. They see
Strider going hand over hand along the rope, moonlight glinting on his crossbow.

ON THE SHORE

Another strand of the rope breaks. We follow it as it unravels - past Diamond and Will. Before we get to Strider it stops - a section of the rope
is so badly frayed it can't go any farther. It's going to break any moment.

Screech! A siren wails.

STRIDER

They've seen us! Will looks up-river to the bridge. Through a hole in the
mist he sees ape guards pointing and yelling. A whole squadron runs to join
them.

Diamond throws herself forward - she makes the shore!

Will and Strider give it everything they've got. Strider's first hand passes the frayed section. He's following it with his second -

229

Snap! The whole rope breaks. Will - closest to the shore - plunges into the
ripping current. But at leaIt he's clinging to the rope with both hands.
Strider's in the water hanging on to the end of the rope by the fingers of
one paw. Will turns and reaches for him.

STRIDER (CONT'D)

No! Save yourselfl

ON THE SHORE

Diamond has grabbed hold of the rope and is trying to pull it in. The
weight - of the men and the current - make it impossible. All she can do is
try and hold them.

ON THE ROPE

Strider's fingers are slipping free. Will grabs him - man and ape, hand to
paw. Will holds him.

STRIDER

Return of the Creatures

We'll both die. Let go! Will shakes his head - no. Hanging on to the rope
one-handed, the current tearing at his body, he tries to haul Strider in.

Whizz! An arrow flies past, just missing them, and plunges into the water.
The apes on the bridge are firing.

STRIDER (CONT'D)

Another minute, we'll both be dead. Do it, Will!

Will tries again to drag Strider to the rope. Another arrow flies through
the mist and spray - even closer. Strider reaches out with his free hand.
He starts to prize Will's fingers loose -

STRIDER (CONT'D)

If nothing else, I made it to the Falls No Return.

Will realizes - nothing is going to stop Strider.

WILL

Return of the Creatures

The sacred words, Strider - what are the words?!

STRIDER

"In the beginning...

WILL

'In the beginning was the word and the word wes God...'

STRIDER

(in wonder)

You know the words?

WILL

You'll walk in the next world, Strider.

STRIDER

How do you know?

WILL

I've seen the future, haven't I?

Strider smiles at him - a smile of perfect peace.

STRIDER

Good-bye Will. Take care of Billie.

Return of the Creatures

He twists Will's last finger free.
He drops - the swirling river carries
him away. Will is close to tears,
but he won't let himself cry. Two more
arrows sizzle past -

WILL

And the word was God. Yea, though I
walk through the valley of death, I
will fear no evil...

Strider spins down the river,
through the spray and foam.

WILL (O.S.) (CONT'D)

Surely goodness and mercy shall
follow me all the days of my life
and I
will dwell in the house of the Lord
forever. Amen.

Strider, one arm raised, plunges
over the Falls.

ON THE BRIDGE

We see who's been coordinating the
firing. It's Drak. Archers are kneeling
on the bridge, trying to sight a
target through the foaming water and

Return of the Creatures

clouds of mist.

Drak, never taking his eyes off of
the river, draws back the massive spring
of his crossbow and reloads.

ON THE SHORE

Diamond ia hauling on the rope,
pulling it in. Will, up to his neck in
water, tows himself along it. His
feet find a footing - he starts to
scramble up the bank. Diamond goes
towards him -

Just for a moment, the mist clears.

ON THE BRIDGE

moment's long enough. Drak's seen
him. In one fluid movement he adjusts his
aim and fires -

ON THE SHORE

Diamond is almost in Will's arms.
Sswhack! The arrow rips into WiU's back,
through his ribs. He pitches
forward. Diamond screams. He falls into her
arms.

The mist closes around them.

Return of the Creatures

HUGE STONE ARCH

The survivors of the Seven Tribes travel fast along a forest trail. All of them are burdened down with possessions, weary from the road - they are leaving the valley.

Kip's Wife and the Old Man are in the lead. They pass through the arch, out into a clearing. In the middle of it is a fire, shadows camped around it -

Kip's wife and the other survivors stop in fear. One of the shadows rises from the. fire. Bathed in moonlight - almost ghost-like - he comes towards them. It's Aragorn!

Kip's wife moves forward and embraces him -

KIP'S WIFE

We thought you were dead.

ARAGORN

Hunted, but not dead. A dozen of us were driven back in the battle -

Return of the Creatures

He indicates his men. They are coming forward, greeting the survivors. The
Young Woman sees her mate - she cries out. They hold each other.

ARAGORN (CONT'D)

For three days a squadron of apes have tracked us. Last night we ambushed
them. We're heading now for the eagle's nest.

KIP'S WIFE

(softly)

There is no eagle's nest.

Aragorn stares at her, not wanting to believe it.

KIP'S WIFE (CONT'D)

We're all that's left of the Seven Tribes.

Grief wells up inside Aragorn. We hold on his face.

A FIRE CRACKLES

All of the tribes-people are gathered around it.

Return of the Creatures

OLD MAN

There is no-one else, Aragorn - you are the Ranger.

ARAGORN

(shaking his head)

No. We must all follow the trail we think best. You've decided yours. For
me * I'll go to the city of the apes and take what revenge I can. I'll go
alone - but like the traveler, I think death will be the only thing I find
there.

OLD MAN

Then it will find us, too. Warriors follow their Ranger. That's always been
the way of it in Middle Earth.

ARAGORN

But nothing's the same now. Think of the women-folk. What will become of
them?

KIP'S WIFE

Return of the Creatures

You're right - there's so few of us now, nothing is the same. You must allow the women to follow, too.

ARAGORN But women can't fight.

KIP'S WIFE Women have never been allowed to fight. That doesn't mean they
can't.

All the women nod their assent. The men smile, agreeing. Everyone waits for
Aragorn to decide. A beat - then he nods his head and smiles.

The tribes-people start to cheer. The Lookout steps forward. From out of
the folds of his fur, he takes the Crescent of Light. All of the tribe stare at it.

LOOKOUT

I found it on the battlefield. There were those who said the Rangers had
left Middle Earth forever - I didn't know what to do with it.

He hands it to Aragorn. The whole tribe watches as the proud man once again
ties the talisman of his rank around his neck.

Return of the Creatures

ARAGORN

Douse the fire. The Seven Tribes are going to war.

ON THE SHORE

The apes, carrying torches, search the river bank and surrounding cliffs.
We push in on a pool of darkness behind them -

Will and Diamond hide in a hollow beneath the tangled roots of a huge tree.
They have done their best to dress Will's wound but he's obviously in a lot
of pain -

DIAMOND

You can't go on, Will - not like this.

WILL

What about the baby?

DIAMOND

I'll keep going - I'll try and get Eve.

WILL

Return of the Creatures

Alone? Don't be ridiculous -

He starts to haul himself to his feet. His face twists in pain - he has to
stop.

DIAMOND

Look at you - you can barely walk.

He puts out his hand, needing I boost up.

WILL

If I can just get up - help me.

Diamond shakes her head - no. They look at one another.

WILL (CONT'D)

Don't do this to me - pleasel

DIAMOND

You've done enough - more than anyone else could. You're one of the finest
men

I've ever known - but it's over, Will. You're going to have to wait. Now
it's my turn -

She grabs her weapons and starts to leave. Will makes it to his feet -

WILL

Billie!She's almost through the tangled roots.

WILL (CONT'D)

I made a mistake once - I went on a journey with someone I loved. At the
end, I let her go into danger alone.

Diamond stops.

DIAMOND

Where was that - Berkeley, Will?

She turns and looks at him. He nods his head - yes.

DIAMOND (CONT'D)

What happened?

WILL

I knew I'd found the chemical key. I was working with three young researchers. One of them was a woman called Ali Conoily. We were engaged.

They were the ones that went into the tanks. I didn't know as much as I
thought I did. They died in there.

DIAMOND

Why didn't you go, Will?

WILL

We all wanted to. It was a great adventure. Wa drew lots for it. I should
never have agreed, but we were young - and like the young we thought life
would last forever.

DIAMOND

Robert Plant died too, didn't he - in a way?

WILL

The experiment was unauthorized. There was an inquiry. They said the theory
had no basis. 'Ludicrous" was a word they used. My career had gone up like
a rocket. It came down like the stick. I couldn't find work anywhere

DIAMOND

Return of the Creatures

"Will Robinson" - that was your joke, I guess. You were Lost in Space, were you?

WILL

Yeah, but I never realized it'd be so appropriate.

They sort of smile at one another.

WILL (CONT'D)

had twenty years to work out where my research went wrong - so what, though. It was just a mind game. But I've learnt a lot of things - the most
important is that sometimes you get a second chance. A second chance for a
lot of things -

He looks straight at her. They hold each other's eyes.

WILL (CONT'D)

And when you do, you have to grab it and make sure you never let it go.
I've got the heart, Billie. It's my body that's failing me.

Neither one of them moves. A beat.

Return of the Creatures

DIAMOND

Give me your hand, Will.

She helps him to his feet.

A GIANT CHASM

It's several hours before dawn. In the gloom - whooshl Kip's Wife rides a
flying fox across a precipitous drop.

She lands on the other side of a jagged ravine. The rest of the tribe, all
heavily armed, are waiting there. They turn end run, fading into the trees.

THE FUNERAL ROCK

juts out into the roaring river. Will and Diamond scramble out of the
darkness and land on the rock. Will's face is haggard with pain but he
forces himself forward. He's loosening up. going faster as he moves -

They pass through the huge legs of the stone ape - into the Temple.

Return of the Creatures

A DARKENED ROOM

Torches flicker on the walls. From somewhere close-by - muffled - we hear
the sound of a crowd. A young ape, barely in his teens, stands in the middle of the room, almost naked. His face is painted with strange ochre
markings.

A circle of ape warriors watch as Ma-Gog lifts a slender blade. Intoning
words in some strange tongue, he slices the blade across the Teenager's
forehead. The Teenager winces but he doesn't cry out - this is his manhood
ceremony.

THE STABLES

The sound of the crowd is much louder here but still we don't see them. The
prisoners from the Eagle's Nest are crowded into the corrals.

One of the gates is thrown open. Three ape guards enter. They push the
tribes-people aside and grab a 12-year old boy. His mother clings to him,

screaming. One of the guards drags her off and they haul the boy out of the
corral.

AN ARENA

-like a small bullring - in the center of the stables. Now we see the crowd
- apes, all males, sit in the bleachers. They roar as a door is opened and
the young Tribe-Boy is pushed into the ring.

He looks around the arena - yelling, screaming apes. Terror on his face. An
even louder roar goes up. The Boy turns -

The Teenage ape steps out of a tunnel, the ochre markings on his face like
war-paint, the blood barely dried on his forehead. He carries spears and a
club.

One of the apes throws a couple of captured human weapons down to the Boy.
The Teenage ape moves in on him. He is a warrior now - this is going to be
his first kill.

Return of the Creatures

IN THE CORRAL

The Boy's mother is huddled down, being comforted by other tribes-people. A
huge roar goes up from the arena as the first blow is struck. The sound carries over to -

A TERRACE

Drak is alone, walking a high ridge. He stops, looking down on the
twinkling lights. The city is virtually deserted but Drak doesn't move -
he's uneasy, troubled by something he can't put a name to.

THE COOL AND LOVELY ROOM

The five baby apes sit on cots. They watch as Doctor Zora inserts a syringe
into the smallest ape's arm. The baby starts to cry. Doctor Zora comforts
her as she draws out a cup of blood. She turns to her assistant, Ben-Guri

DOCTOR ZORA

Is the girl animal ready?

Return of the Creatures

BEN-GURI

They're doing it now.

INSIDE THE LABORATORY

Eve is struggling and crying as an ape guard carries her towards an operating table. He and another guard start to strap her down.

The Vet works at the bench, heating a steel needle over a flame. It's the
same sort of catheter that was used on Will - one end of the needle attached to a long tube. A knock on the door.

VET

That must be Zors with the blood.

One of the guards goes and unbolts the door. He recoils - it's Will. Sswhack! He fires the first bolt from a double-barreled crossbow. It takes
the guard in the chest.

He and Diamond dive into the room. Eve starts hollering. The second guard
is wheeling, crossbow rising. He rifle-butts Diamond across the head. Her
weapon goes flying.

Return of the Creatures

The guard is aiming. Will is on the floor, tumbling. Barely time to aim, on
his back, firing overhead, he shoots -

Whack! Bullseye. The arrow hits the guard dead in the heed.

The Vet grabs the first guard's fallen crossbow. He aims at Will. Diamond
screams a warning but there's nothing Will can do - he's struggling to
reload, one-handed because of his wounds.

Diamond - unarmed - scoops the red-hot syringe off the bench. The Vet
reaches for the trigger. Diamond leaps forward. She drives the syringe into
his chest.

The Vet stands goggle-eyed. Diamond must have found his heart - a torrent
of blood pours down the clear tube. It spills on to the floor. The Vet
topples forward.

Slash! Slash! Will cuts throughthe straps that tie Eve to the table.

OUTSIDE THE HALL OF LEARNING

Return of the Creatures

Drak turns a corner of the building. He stops and touches the ground with
his finger. He lifts it to his mouth and tastes it. He rises to his feet,
following trail of blood.

A TORCH

is ripped from a bracket. It's Drak.. He shines it down into a stone well.
The flame splits the darkness. Floating in the water at the bottom of the
well is an ape guard -dead, an arrow through his throat.

IN THE ARENA

The Tribe-Boy is sprawled in the dust, bleeding badly from a rip across his
ribs. His spear lies next to him, a wooden shield raised across his head.
The Teenage ape , rains blows down on it with a sword.

The apes in the bleachers are cheering wildly. Smash! The shield splinters.
The sword slices the Boy's arm -

APES

Return of the Creatures

Kill! Kill! Kill!

The Boy stares up - the Teenage smiles and raises his sword.

Shriek! The alarm sounds.
Everything freezes. Then officers are on their
feet, yelling orders. Ape soldiers grab their weapons, heading for the doors.

The Teenage ape looks around, robbed of his moment. The Boy sees his
chance. He raises his spear and drives it deep into the ape's groin. He
staggers and falls - on top of the Boy.

The apes pour out of the arena. The siren carries over to -

A STONE CORRIDOR

Will's got Eve slung over his shoulder. They're stumbling down a corridor -
past other labs and research rooms. They burst through a sat of doors, into
-

A COURTYARD

Return of the Creatures

at the back of the Hall of Learning. It's deep in shadow. From behind they
hear the sound of pounding feet. Will looks around, not sure which way to
go. He glances across a terrace - the doors to the stables fly open. The
ape warriors charge out.

WILL

Can you ride?

Diamond nods her head - yes. He thrusts Eve into her hands -

WILL (CONT'D)

Go for the stables. Head for the eagle's nest. I'll try to join you there.

Diamond hesitates - she doesn't want to leave him.

DIAMOND

What are you going to do?

WILL

Delay them. Now go, Billie. Go!

THE PRIMITIVE ELEVATOR

rops down the side of the ravine.
Standing on it are Nazgul and about

THE PRIMITIVE ELEVATOR

a dozen Praetorian Guards. Nazgul
looks down - torches and fires in
drums
are lighting up the streets and
terraces. Ape soldiers are running
everywhere - searching.

ON THE GROUND

The flame-thrower rolls along a
street. The driver's canopy is
hidden by
flapping tarpaulins. In the chaos
nobody pays it any attention.

ON THE ELEVATOR

Nazgul sees the machine rolling
towards them.

NAZGUL

That's strange - why does Drak need
the Flame?

Suddenly he realizel. He turns,
screaming up at the apes
controlling the
mechanism.

NAZGUL (CONT'D)

Return of the Creatures

Stop! Take it back!

THE FLAME-THROWER

dead guard is draped over the side
of the machine, blood dripping from his
headWill is in the cabin, working
the controls. He sees the elevator slow
in mid-descent. He throws a lever
forward. For a moment, nothing.
Then -

Whoosh! A huge tongue of flame
blasts out of the barrel.

Two of the guards are trying to
climb the ropes. Nazgul is wheeling around
in a panic. The flame hits them!
The whole wooden structure catches fire.
We see the apes through the flames,
struggling and writhing.

The ropes burn through. The blazing
structure plummets down -

THE CENTRAL SQUARE

Smash! It hits the ground in a
shower of blazing timbers and dead apes. Ape
soldiers - standing nearby - stare
in shock. The smell of roasted ape fills

the air.

EVE SITS ALONE

She's on the floor of the stables, deep in shadow. She's scared, looking
ahead -

The first weak light of dawn shines through the open doors. We see an ape
guard, keys jangling from his waist, on petrol.

He hears something - a rock falling, a rustle of movement. Raising his
weapon, he moves towards a pool of black shadow, past a pile of rocks, into
an alcove.

Diamond rises out of the rocks behind him. He spins - she's got her
cross-bow raised. Point-blank range. She nails him.

THE PRISONERS

are shackled in the corrals. They see Diamond running out of the shadows
towards them. She tossel them the keys -

Return of the Creatures

DIAMOND

Arm yourselves. Find Will - he needs youl She turns and goes. The prisoners
start to unlock the chains.

EVE

smiles as Diamond races out of the shadows, sweeps her up and keeps running.

IN THE ARENA

The Teenage ape and the Boy lie where they fell, their spilt blood staining
the dust.

The Boy's mother scrambles over the deserted bleachers and goes to her son.
She drags off the ape. Her son's eyes are closed, his arms lacerated, his
chest wounded and crusted with blood. She stares at him - he doesn't move.

She starts to sob. The Boy's eyes flicker open. They look at one another.
The motheY gathers him into her arms. He's alive! He's alive!

Return of the Creatures

The sound of a horse. The mother turns, fearful. She looks across the
arena, through a railing -

IN THE CORRALS

Diamond gallops a stallion through the corrals. Eve's clutching the saddle
in front of her - hair flying, her eyes sparkling with exhilaration. The
stallion gallops faster.

The prisoners - unchaining the last of their comrades - turn and look. It's
a magnificent sight. Diamond is crouched low over the flying horse. Straight ahead - a railed fence, part of the corral.

She leaps the horse over it. They land. In front - another hurdle. Again
she does it.

The prisoners stare. Diamond charges towards the open doors of the stables.

CLOUDS OF SMOKE AND FLAME

The crashed elevator hal set the surrounding buildings on fire. Ape city is

Return of the Creatures

burning.

The Flame stands on a steep incline, its back wedged against the wall of a
terrace. Whooshl Fire shoots out of its barrel as Will keeps a horde of ape
soldiers at bay.

The soldiers turn - Drak, surrounded by the Praetorian Guard, gallops
straight towards them. He'l not stopping for anything - the soldiers
scramble aside.

IN THE CABIN

Will sees Drak and the guards appear through the swirling clouds of smoke.
They look like the horsemen of the apocalypse. As Will throws the lever we
sea a primitive gauge above his head. It's in the red -

IN THE SQUARE

Whoosh! The tongue of flame shoots through the smoke. It touches the guards
with a deadly kiss, throwing them screaming from their horses. But Drak

blasts through -

IN THE CABIN

Will is engulfed in a backdraft of black oily smoke. He peers through it -
Drak charges towards him! Will hits the lever again. The flame erupts from
the barrel. Then it dies - out of fuel.

WILL

Shit!

IN THE SQUARE

Drak gallops forward. He raises weapon - a shoulder-mounted harpoon. He
aims -

IN THE CABIN

Will throws himself aside. He smashes both hands down on a lever on the
floor. A hiss of steam. The machine lurches forward -

IN THE SQUARE

Drak tries to get a clear shot at Will. The machine gathers speed down the

incline, coming straight towards Drak. He veers his horse aside and wheels
around. He charges alongside the cabin - it's empty

ON THE MACHINE

Will clings to the outside of the Flame as it roars across the smoke-filled
square. He's out of sight of Drak - but not for long. The ape and his stallion loom into view behind the machine, Will scrambles back into the
cabin -

IN THE SQUARE

Apes are scattering as the runaway machine flies across the square. Drak is
at full gallop, veering from one side of the Flame to the other. Will
clambers back and forth - cat and mouse at full tilt.

Drak swings his horse close to the back of the machine. He stands up in the
stirrups, the harpoon clamped to his shoulder - he's going on board!

Return of the Creatures

The Flame flies out of the square and down a street. An ape throws himself
into a doorway - just in time, Drak steadies himself, about to jump. Suddenly his horse whinnies wildly. Drak looks ahead - holy shit!. They're
heading straight for the front of a blazing house.

Drak throws himself down into the saddle and hauls on the reins. Will hurls
himself back into the cabin, arms shielding his head. Smash! The Flame
crashes through the front wall -

INSIDE THE HOUSE

The barrel of the Flame acts like a battering ram - it blasts through the
walls in a shower of burning timbers. It crashes through the kitchen and
stops in a courtyard.

Will clambers out of the cabin and drops to the ground. A yell goes up -
apes are coming through the adjoining houses. Will turns and heads down an
alleyway.

Return of the Creatures

CITY STREET

Diamond's horse flies down a street - a high terrace towers on one side, a
row of burning buildings on the other. The road turns right. She swings
around it - apes! A platoon of them right in front of her. She screams at
Eve -

DIAMOND

Hold on!

She throws herself aside, pulling on the reins. The horse spins in a
U-turn, grazing past a burning building. Diamond gallops back the way she
came.

Crash! The wall of a burning building in front of her collapses. Blazing
beams block the road. The horse shies away. Diamond wheels him around -

The apes race into the road. She looks around desperately - she's trapped.
She grabs Eve and awingl her onto the saddle behind her - she'll be safer

Return of the Creatures

there.

She spurs the horse forward and
crouches Iow in the saddle - she's going to
charge straight through the apes.
They drop to one knee - the firing
position - and raise their weapons.
A dozen crossbowl aim straight at
Diamond.

There's no way out - she flies
towards them. Whizzl The sound of
arrows.
But it's not the apes - they go
down like nine-pins.

Diamond looks up - Aragorn has
arrived! Backlit by the rising sun, the men
and women of the Tribes are pouring
volley after volley into the apes.
Nobody fires better than Kip's
Wife.

Diamond leaps the horse through the
dead and dying apes and turns down the
road.

MA-GOG

stands on a terrace, his cloak
blowing in the wind, his one cruel eye
blazing with anger. Flanked by two
ape warriors, he looks down on the

Return of the Creatures

burning buildings.

The freed prisoners are waging a pitched battle outside the stables.

Ma-Gog sees Will - he's running along the rooftops, leaping from one
building to the next. Ma-Gog points at him, yelling at apes in the streets
below -

MA-GOG (CONT'D)

Kill him! In the name of God, kill himl Sswhish! The blade of a sword cleaves through frame. It cuts one of the ape warriors from neck to waist.
Ma-Gog spins - it's Aragorn, armed to the teeth, behind them.

The second warrior goes for him. Aragorn has dropped the sword. He raises a
crossbow and fires. The bolt shatters the ape's armor and buries itself in
his chest.

Ma-Gog swirls aside his cloak. In his good hand he holds a double-edged
sword. Aragorn drops the crossbow ands ducks beneath Ma-Gog's arcing blow.

Return of the Creatures

He lunges with a short-handled spear -

ARAGORN

For my people!

It takes Ma-Gog in the gut. His one eye bulges. Aragorn rips the spear out -

ARAGORN (CONT'D)

And this - for my daughterl He drives the spear into the High Priest's
heart. The cruel eye flickers and dies.

ON THE ROOFTOP

Will has seen it all. He screams -

WILL

Behind you! Aragorn - behind!

ON THE TERRACE

Aragorn turns. It's Drak, on horseback, thundering down on him. But the
leader of the Seven Tribes knows no fear - only the memory of his lost child.

Return of the Creatures

He raises his second spear and charges straight at Drak. The huge ape
levels the shoulder-mounted harpoon. He pulls the trigger. Sswang! The
powerful spring on the barrel releases, the harpoon trails a length of rope
behind it -

Wham! The harpoon smashes through Aragorn's chest. He dies as he falls.

ON THE ROOFTOP

Will stares in anguish. He turns away - he sees Diamond. She's at full
gallop - Eve clinging to her back - charging along a road several terraces
below. She's got a clear run for the iron bridge and freedom.

Will looks across at Drak - he's seen her too! For a moment the two of them
stare at one another. Will's face is drawn and haggard from the injuries he
carries.

Drak's lip curls in a sneer - he knows he's going to win. He beats his

chest with his fists and spurs the
stallion over the edge of the
terrace,
going for Diamond.

Will runs as fast as his body will
let him - along the rooftop.

INSIDE A HOUSE

An ape mother cowers in a corner,
her two children clutched to her,
the
sounds of battle all around. She
looks up in terror -

Smash! Will's feet blast through
the roof. He lands on the floor,
crossbow
raised -but not st her. Framed in
the front doorway is an ape warrior
on
horseback. Wham! Will shoots him
and runs for the horse.

DIAMOND

and Eve fly down charred street
.They head towards a large open
square.

OUTSIDE THE STABLES

Smoke and dust swirl through the
air. The freed prisoners are
fighting ape

infantry. Drak races past the battle. The rope from the harpoon is tied
around the saddle, dragging Aragorn's body through the dust.

He looks ahead - Diamond gallops across the square. Drak whips his horse
forward -

A CURVED ROAD

on a high terrace. Flying around a corner - Will! His coat is billowing,
the horse's mane streaming in the wind. He hits the straight-away and gallops even faster.

He looks down on the road below - Diamond is ahead but Drak is gaining on
her. Will plunges into a tunnelhewn out of rock.

ON THE ROAD

Eve clings tight to Diamond's waist. The little girl looks back - Drak is
thundering behind them, pennants snapping in the wind, armor glinting on
the horse's chest. It's an awesome sight.

Return of the Creatures

Drak has the reins in his teeth.
He's using both hands to reload the
harpoon.

Diamond sees the bridge dead ahead.
Heavily armed apes have barricaded
it.
She curses and yanks the bridle.
The horse sweeps around an island
in the
center of the road - a huge
monument to some dead ape. She
gallops back the
way she came, almost passing Drak.
He charges round the island.

OUT OF THE TUNNEL

comes Will. He looks down to the
lower road - Diamond and Drak are
coming
back towards him! He turns the
horse around - back into the
tunnel.

Whooshl He flies out the other end,
into daylight. He looks over his
shoulder - he's in front of them
but thirty feet too high. He digs
his
heels into the horse's flanks -over
a Iow wall they fly. God knows
where it
goes -

DOWN A ROCKY SUDE

into a dead-end cul-de-sac just above the roadway. Apesi Two of them are
guarding the Claw and the Bells. Will fires from the shoulder - he drops
the first ape.

The second ape aims at him. Will raises another crossbow. They fire almost
simultaneously. Will throws himself aside, out of the saddle. The horse rears and bolts.

Will looks up from the dirt - the ape has Will's arrow embedded in his
chest. He falls forward - dead.

Will scrambles to a parapet and looks down on the road just below. Diamond
and Eve - clinging to the horse for dear life - race towards him. Will grabs a crossbow and struggles to reload. He can't - it takes the strength
of both arms to cock it,

ON THE ROAD

Diamond's horse is lathered in sweat, almost blown. Eve looks over her

shoulder, her eyes wide with fear -
Drak is close behind, gaining at every
step.

IN THE CUL-DE-SAC

Will leaps from the Balls on to the Claw.

ON THE ROAD

Drak swings the harpoon on to his shoulder. He sights down the barrel. Eve
sees the weapon lock on to their backs. She screams a warning et Diamond -

EVE

Billie!

Diamond leaps the horse over a charred wagon abandoned on the road. Drak
loses her in his sights. He follows her over the wagon.

ON THE CLAW

Will is in the driver's seat. He throws a lever - nothing happens. He tries
another -the long jib that supportl the two iron jews swings towards the

Return of the Creatures

road.

DRAK

aims the harpoon. He's got Eve end Diamond, one behind the other, in his
sights.

DRAK

A bargain - two for the price of one!

ON THE CLAW

Will spins a small steering wheel.

ON THE ROAD

Drak is close behind Diamond. The harpoon's massive spring is coiled. Drak's finger curls around the trigger, about to fire.

Suddenly he screams - dropping right in front, coming straight towards him,
are the opening jaws of the Claw.

WILL JERKS BACK ANOTHER LEVER -

WILL

Keep your hands off her, you dirty ape.

Return of the Creatures

The jaws lock clean around Drak's
waist, plucking him off the saddle
and
lifting him up into the air. He's
still got the harpoon. He sees Will
at
the control. He swings the barrel
round -

Will hits a switch. Wrong one -
nothing happens.

Drak's got him in his sights. His
finger finds the trigger -

Will throws another switch.

The jaws start to close! Drak tries
to pull the trigger - he can't, his
body is twisting. The jaws are
crushing him! He musters all of his
strength
and tries to fire. He and Will look
straight at one another. A beat.
Drsk's
finger starts to slide off the
trigger -

IN THE SQUARE

Apes stare up at their warrior
lord, clamped in the Clew. He let
out a
blood curdling scream. The bottom
half of his torso - everything from
the

Return of the Creatures

waist down - falls towards the
ground. Maybe it's just the wind,
but the
legs still seem to be kicking.

The apes reel beck in horror. With
mighty battle cry, the tribes-
people -
the prisoners end Aregom'l
followers - hurl themselves
forward, attacking.

The apes break end start to run.

ON THE ROAD

Diamond end Eve have dismounted.
Diamond stumbles forward - Will is
coming
towards her. She holds out her arms
and they embrace. Neither one says
a
word, they just hold each other
tight.

CLOUDS OF SMOKE

almost obscure the setting sun.
Will and Diamond stand on the iron
bridge
watching the tribes-people. They've
harnessed horses to ropes tied
around
the statues on the avenue of idols
- one after another the stone
monoliths
come crashing down.

DIAMOND

If nothing else, we helped the tribes take back their valley.

WILL

Our valley, too Billia.

She looks at him - questioning.

WILL (CONT'D)

There's one thing I never told you - I never worked out how to get back.

She smiles at him.

DIAMOND

A small point. But give me some credit. I'm a scientist - I knew that.

WILL

(in wonder)

But you came anyway.

DIAMOND

That was love.

WILL

For the baby?

She shakes her head.

DIAMOND

For the both of you.

They stare into each other's eyes.
They kiss.

DIAMOND (CONT'D)

I only have one regret. We'll never
know if we succeeded.

WILL

Of course we will. You're pregnant
- if the baby's born alive, we'll
know
it worked.

SUNLIGHT GLISTENS ON THE OCEAN

The surf rolls in on a golden
beach. At the water's edge, a line
of
footprints. We follow them to find
Will on top of a rocky cliff. He's
building something out of iron and
rock and sand but we can't make out
what
it is.

DIAMOND (O.S.)

Return of the Creatures

Willl He turns and runs to the mouth of a large cave.

INSIDE THE CAVE

Diamond lies on her back on a pile of animal skins. Her belly is exposed,
heaw with the unborn child. Eve crouches next to her, trying to help.

WILL

It's started?

She nods her head then grimaces with pain as another contraction starts.

THE SUN IS SETTING ON THE SEA

From inside the cave, we hear Diamond scream.

IN THE CAVE

Will kneels between Diamond's legs. Her face, glistening with sweat; is a
mask of pain. She holdl Eve's hind tight and pushes.

Will, half hidden by her upraised legs, delivers the child. Diamond raises

Return of the Creatures

herself up -trying to See her child. Neither she nor us can see it's face.

We push in on Will. Ha raises his hand and slaps the baby's rump. No sound.
Ha raises his hand again - suddenly the baby starts to cry. Now we see the
baby - a perfect little boy.

Eve laughs. Diamond smiles. Tears fill her eyes. She and Will look at one
another. He comes towards her and tenderly places the baby in her arms.

THE CAVE

Will and Eve help Diamond. She comes out of the cave, still holding the
baby. It's magic hour - they stand on a rock ledge, looking at the ocean
washed with colour from the setting sun.

We see what Will was building. It's sort of like a sculpture - just the head and crown of the Statue of Liberty.

Diamond smiles. She looks at him, wondering why -

Return of the Creatures

WILL

It's to make sure we never forget where we came from.

The baby starts to cry. Will puts one arm each around Diamond and Eve.

We pull back from them - high up into the stars. The baby's cry carries
over. We see earth rise. In all this nothingness - life.

Printed in Great Britain
by Amazon